SHADOWS OF THE PAST

The Cassie Tam Files, Book Four

Matt Doyle

A NineStar Press Publication

Published by NineStar Press
P.O. Box 91792,
Albuquerque, New Mexico, 87199 USA.
www.ninestarpress.com

Shadows of the Past

Printed in the USA
First Edition
November, 2019

Print ISBN: 978-1-951057-76-3

Also available in eBook, ISBN: 978-1-951057-70-1

Warning: This book contains bullying, stalking, a deceased family member, guns, and workplace harassment. This book is part of a series and needs to be read in sequence.

Shadows of the Past is the new novella collection set in The Cassie Tam Files universe! Enjoy two new stories that follow PI Cassie Tam and her girlfriend Lori Redwood as they deal with the fallout from LV48. This book is part of a series and needs to be read in sequence.

A Week in New Hopeland

When Lori Redwood agrees to help out her girlfriend, PI Cassie Tam, by going undercover at a local shipping firm, she gets more than she bargained for. Her 'boss' Mr. Graves is a misogynist and a bully, and has been targeting one girl in particular. Cassie is known to him, and he tends to be cautious around Tech Shifters. Which means that Lori may be the best person for the job.

Will Lori be able to help Cassie gather enough evidence for the police to act, or will she become the next target?

Shadows of the Past

PI Cassie Tam is not the only person who lives with regrets, and like most people, she just wants to get on with her life. But in New Hopeland, the past *never* remains buried. When she's hired to track a stalker that's been using some interesting tech to mask their identity on the city's security cameras, Cassie ends up face-to-face with her darkest memory.

Can Cassie find out who's responsible before her past mistakes tear her—and her friends—apart?

Table of Contents

A WEEK IN NEW HOPELAND

Chapter One

LORI

I roll over in bed and let my arm flop into the empty space next to me. Even with my eyes closed, I can tell the early morning light is beginning to creep in through the window. My slightly bent leg finds a long warm spot, giving away that Cassie hasn't been up long. I instinctively grip the bedsheet where her body would normally end and let out a content sigh.

"Mine," I say to myself and roll onto my back again. I raise my hands to my face and rub the sleep out of my eyes, taking in the familiar sight of my bedroom as I clear the cobwebs a little. There are other things to wake me up too; new things that are becoming more familiar as time passes. Smells and sounds I don't experience as often as I'd like. But I have to be careful, gentle even. Cassie is outwardly quite rough, but she's softer on the inside. She's like an emotional armadillo.

A partial conversation from last night flashes across my mind, and a smile reaches my lips. I sit up and stretch, forcing out a yawn as I glance at the back of the door. "Someone's borrowing my robe again."

I grab my spare from the wardrobe and tie it up, then walk down the hall, through the living room, and up to the kitchen. I rest against the doorframe, watching Cassie as she carries on oblivious to my presence. After a moment, I say, "Morning."

Cassie jumps a little and smiles my way. She pulls gently at the sleeve of the robe and says, "Sorry, I didn't bring mine. I wasn't planning to stay over, but…"

"Ink can be quite persuasive, can't she?" I nod to the frying pan on the hob and ask, "What'cha cooking?"

Cassie's lips tighten and her nose wrinkles, making her look like a cute, frustrated, pouting bunny. She taps the bowl she's been piling the food in. "It was supposed to be pancakes. I don't know what went wrong, I'm normally really good with pancakes. These keep sticking, though. And burning. Maybe I didn't use enough oil."

"Nah, it'll be the pan," I reply, walking into the room and grabbing some plates from the cupboard. "And they look fine, just a little broken."

"The pan, eh?"

"Yup. That one never was much good. *Everything* sticks to it, no matter what you do."

"Huh. If it's that bad, why keep it?"

"Sentimental reasons," I reply and start splitting the pancakes out. "So, come on, detective, see if you can figure it out."

"The first thing you bought for here?" she tries.

I hand her a plate and shake my head. "Nope. Try again."

"A gift from a relative?"

"Swing and a miss," I say and start pouring us a drink from the percolator she's been keeping warm in preparation. "One more guess."

She shrugs and grabs two forks from the drawer. She hands me one as she answers, "You got me."

We walk to the living room and sit on the couch. "Well, a few years back, I was woken up by this noise in the kitchen. It must have been about three in the morning,

I think. Anyway, I started panicking, right? *There's someone in the house. Who is it? What do they want?* That sort of thing.

"Well, we'd been covering some home break-in stories at work, and I decided there and then I wasn't going to be just another victim, sitting scared in my room while someone takes all my stuff. So, I got up, and creeped up to the kitchen as quietly as I could, and what did I find? Someone going through the fridge."

"Who was it?"

"I couldn't tell. Between tiredness, the darkness, and the fridge door being slightly closed, I couldn't see anything at all really, other than a silhouette. So, I grabbed the first sturdy thing I could."

"The frying pan."

"Exactly. I grabbed it, waited for them to step back, and swung. *Bam.*"

"Then what happened?"

"The woman dropped her milk and starts yelling, 'What the fuck, Lori?' So, I turn the light on, and everything starts slotting into place. I'd been out at a club and taken this lady home. Karen, I think her name was. The problem was, I'd gotten a bit drunk and, between that and the stories we'd been covering, I'd completely forgotten she'd stayed over and had gotten a little paranoid."

"Was she all right?" Cassie asks, staring at me in disbelief.

"She was angry more than anything. That was our one and only night together, though. But yeah, so the frying pan is sentimental for me because it reminds me that one, I shouldn't bring people home if I met them while drunk, and two, I'm not as much of as a wuss as I thought."

Cassie laughs. "I guess I should be happy you didn't think I was an intruder, eh?"

I smile and kiss her forehead. "*You* never need to worry. If I wake up and you're gone, I'll just assume you're off dealing with any intruder. And even if I *did* somehow forget you were staying over, I can always tell when you're in the kitchen in the morning. You sing while you cook."

Cassie stops mid-sip, and her eyes go wide, peering over the top of the mug. "*Diu.* You can hear that?"

"'Iris' by the Goo Goo Dolls, wasn't it? I mean, it's clearly a product of its era, but it's a good track."

"Oh, no, no, no. You weren't meant to hear that. It's why I stop when I hear your bedroom door open."

I tilt my head and frown. "Really? I like it. You sound happy."

"I *am* happy, but...I don't really sing...well. Or in front of people."

"Oh," I reply, a little worried now. "Sorry, I wasn't thinking. I didn't really notice you stopped. I always get excited to see what you're making, so it never really occurred to me."

"It's fine," she says, but I can tell she's still embarrassed. "Anyway, it can't be that exciting. I only use what you have in."

"I know, but I don't always bother myself. Usually, it's cereal or toast if it's just me. Work, right?"

Cassie's shoulders relax a little and she takes another mouthful of coffee. "Oh, I get that. I'm the same at the apartment, really. I don't usually stay here when I have a case on, so there's rarely any rush for me in the morning when I do. I do try to get up early, though, just in case you need to head out earlier. I can make sure I still get something made for you then."

I take a leaf from Cassie's playbook and fail to stop the blush rising to my cheeks. If she enjoys doing it, I may as well tell her. "Okay, confession time. Sometimes, I buy a few things I know I might not have the time to cook. You know, to see if you use them when you stop over. I kinda might have noticed you enjoy cooking more than you let on. And, you know, I quite like what you put in front of me."

I take another big mouthful of pancake to prove the point, and Cassie giggles. "Well, aren't you full of surprises today?"

"Oh, speaking of surprises, it's the Saturday after next, right? Your birthday?"

She rolls her eyes. "Yes, it is. Look, Lori, I really don't want you to make a big deal out of it. Just something small, eh?"

I wave my hands frantically, spilling a little coffee on my knee. Good job it's cooled down. "Absolutely. I promised I wouldn't go overboard, so I won't. We'll do a stop at a café. And maybe a present or two."

"No more than two," she says, fixing me with a stern look.

"No more than two," I reiterate.

"And a limit of one hundred dollars."

"I know, I know. You never did explain why you don't like doing too much."

Cassie sighs and puts her empty mug down. "Okay, I guess I owe you that much at least. If you really have to know, my birthday falls exactly one week before...one week before *the anniversary*."

Cassie's dad was a cop back in Canada. He took a bullet for her during her last major case back there, and his death tore her and her mom apart. That was why she moved to New Hopeland. "I'm sorry. I knew it was coming up, but the connection didn't click."

She waves it away, and her walls come up a little. "It's fine; I never told you the date. Honestly, if I didn't want to do anything at all, I wouldn't have told you my birthday either."

"Are you sure?"

"Yeah."

"Just don't be a Nancy, okay?"

"A Nancy?"

"My nan. She *hated* having a fuss made on her birthday, like at all. But she never told us because she didn't want to disappoint anyone. It wasn't until she was at death's door that she finally came clean. Don't be like her. If it's too much, tell me so I can back off."

Cassie's face softens a little and she pulls me into a gentle kiss. "Thank you. It means a lot knowing you'd do that. It's fine; just keep it low key. Anyway, I better get a wash and head back home. You never know when the next case will drop in your lap."

She gets to her feet and starts walking to the door, but I can't help myself. "An armadillo."

She stops. "What?"

"Last night. You asked what sort of animal I thought you'd be if you were a Tech Shifter? Well, I've decided. An armadillo."

"An armadillo," she repeats. "Why?"

I gather the plates and mugs and give her a wink. "I'll let *you* figure that one out."

I DO LIKE the way we run the New Hopeland News Site office. We all have our main jobs, of course, but when we're not on assignment, we pick up the other bits too. To a point, we all learn pretty much every side of the business. The downside is I can sometimes get some pretty dull jobs on non-assignment days.

Click. Click. Click.

Like formatting articles on a cumbersome piece of software a cut below the freeware I use at home. Still, shrinking areas and repositioning images is at least warmer than when they send me out on rainy day jobs to photograph politicians doing their verbal gymnastics for the voters.

Ring-ring.

I pick up the phone and answer with a sort-of-cheery, "NHNS, you're through to Lori Redwood."

"Lori. Hi."

I smile and sit back in my chair. "Hi, Cassie. Missing me already?"

"I always miss you," she says, but there's a noticeable rush to her words. "Listen, your boss, what was his name?"

"Damien Forbes. Cassie, what's wrong? You sound upset."

She sighs. "Sorry. I'm angry, that's all. Is there any chance you could get me a meeting with him?"

"Sure, I'd think so. When for?"

"Today."

I sit forward and start saving my work. "Give me a moment and I'll check. Sounds important."

"Yeah, it is. I, uh, I need you there too. Would that be okay?"

I frown and stop my mouse clicking for a moment. "I don't see why I couldn't be; it's not like I'm on assignment today. Why, though?"

"Not on the phone. I'll explain everything when I'm there if you can sort the meeting out."

"Okay, hang on." I cover the receiver with my hand and lean back. I spot my boss over at his desk a few places along from me, so I shout, "Hey, Forbes. Can you come here for a minute?"

He shoots me a quizzical look but stands up, straightens his, and tie then walks over. "What's up?"

"I've got Cassie Tam on the phone."

"That PI you're—"

"Yeah, that one," I cut in. "She wants to meet with you today, and she wants me there. Any chance?"

He crosses his arms and exhales a gruff grunt. It makes him sound annoyed, but I've known him long enough to know it's a good sign. "Any idea what it's about?"

"She won't say over the phone."

His lips twitch a little and he holds his hand out, beckoning me to hand him the phone. I do so and he says, "Miss Tam, this is Damien Forbes. Look, I'm happy to meet with you, but I need at least something to go on here...yes...uh-huh...okay, how quick can you get here?"

Finally, he nods and puts the phone down. "Sounds like you got more out of her than I did," I say.

"I doubt it. I still don't know what she wants to talk about exactly, just what she wants."

"Which is?"

"Mutual back scratching, apparently. You want to go put your face on or whatever if your girlfriend's coming?"

I feign being mortified and reply, "Are you saying my face needs work? That's workplace bullying, you know."

He flips me the bird and walks away with a "Lock your screen this time, ya cyborg."

WE ONLY HAVE two meeting rooms in the office. One is technically the kitchen, but people congregate there enough that it's been dubbed the "meeting room with food in." The one we're using is a little more standard. Damien has taken the seat behind a small table, and I'm in a chair to the side.

When Cassie arrives, I can tell straight away that whatever's happened, she's taking it very seriously. She gives me a small smile and then takes the chair opposite me, avoiding the one to my right. I expected that. She's in full-on work mode now, which means a need to see both of us combined with some professional distance. I've done the same with friends before, so I know how awkward it probably is for her.

"Thank you for agreeing to meet with me," she says and pulls out her tablet. She loads up a file and says, "If you could both read and sign this, we can begin. It's a confidentiality release, confirming that whether you choose to help or not, you won't discuss anything we talk about outside this room."

Damien skim reads the document and signs. I go ahead and sign without reading. I trust Cassie, and I trust my boss, so I don't see the need to add time to the process.

Cassie nods and takes the tablet back. "I'll get right to it. Have either of you heard of FS Solutions Limited?"

Damien lets out a low, short laugh. "Fast Ship, yeah, I know them. Screwed up our computer order a few months back. They say they'll ship anything, and they probably will, but their definition of fast differs to mine."

"They don't just deal with the shipping," Cassie adds. "They deal with some of the logistics for their clients, too, if they use multiple services to provide goods. They aren't big by New Hopeland standards, but they earn a fair profit."

"Okay, what about them?" Damien asks.

Cassie takes a deep breath and exhales slowly. "I was visited today by one of their office employees. I'm withholding her name for now, but she wasn't in a good way. She works in one of the departments dealing with shifting tasks around to the various staff members. They're seen as a bit of a limbo division; not quite full-blown HR, not quite *not* full-blown HR. It's mostly simple work, but complaints relating to delays or misdirected processes come back on them too."

"Sounds stressful," I say.

"It is, but it's being made worse by her manager. He's started targeting her. It was verbal abuse initially, trying to break her down after she stood up for a colleague he'd been harassing. Once he noticed how scared she was of him, it moved on to physical intimidation. Slamming cups, throwing papers, sticking his finger in her face, that sort of thing. Yesterday..." Cassie raises her hand to her left cheek. "This is where he hit her. He'd offered to take her to dinner to *apologize* for his bad mood, and she declined."

I blink. "Shit. Has she reported him?"

Cassie shakes her head. "She's too scared to. You see, she's not his first victim. Before they shifted to the current business model, they traded as a sort of business intermediary, dealing with the communications and HR management for small start-ups. She can't remember the name they used back then, but this guy apparently did the same thing to another girl. She *did* report him and ended up fired. The whole thing was swept under the carpet by senior management. When she tried taking it to the police, they found the company had conveniently misplaced everything they could have used as evidence."

"That's not normal procedure these days," Damien says. "Who is this guy?"

"Lewis Graves, son of Ted Graves, owner of Fast Ship Limited."

Damien takes his thick-rimmed glasses off and gives them a quick polish on his tie. "Ah, the boss's son. So, Daddy covers it up and he gets to do whatever he wants."

"But what about the other staff?" I ask. "Didn't any of them come forward?"

I shake my head. "They were all too scared to say anything in case they became the next target. When the company changed what they were doing, two of them ended up in his new team. They outright told my client they were sorry, but they couldn't help."

Damien sits back in his chair and crosses his arms behind his head. "Okay, so why this meeting?"

Cassie rests her elbows on the table and crosses her hands, then rests her chin onto them. "I have a plan to make sure this doesn't go *much* further."

"*Much* further?" I repeat, making it a question.

She nods. "The only way this gets resolved is if the police can be given something irrefutable. What I want to do is get a video of him doing what he does. My client would do it, but hidden cameras have an inherent problem."

"The footage is inadmissible in New Hopeland legal cases unless the person being filmed had given their permission to be filmed," Damien replies, scratching his scruffily spiked hair. "In which case, there'd be no need for the camera to be hidden unless it was some reality TV show or something."

"Exactly. I figured if someone like NHNS approached them to film a documentary about New Hopeland businesses, then they'd sign a clause allowing you access to film wherever and whoever you wanted."

Damien drops his arms and crosses them across his chest. "Maybe. But that would mean having the camera on show, and he isn't going to kick off in those circumstances. Nor are the other staff suddenly going to loosen their lips."

"No, but my client has a friend in HR. If you apply for three press passes but intentionally fudge the dates on one to allow someone full access for a week, we could get them added to the team for that period. Said person could then use hidden cameras to catch Mr. Graves digging his own."

Damien snorts a laugh at that, but I'm confused now, so I decide to just come out with it. "Cassie, why did you ask for me to be present?"

She looks away for a moment and steels herself, then replies, "Normally, I'd do the filming for something like this myself. The problem is, even if we ignore the fact I'm not employed here, she knows her boss knows who I am. Remember the press conference I did with the PD during the LV case? He was watching and commenting on it during office hours. It sounds like I'm not his favorite person. He didn't much care for me being as prominent as Captain Hoover, seeing as I'm not a real detective in his eyes. It's a dangerous role, but...okay. My client is the third victim. The second was a girl named Laura. When he hit her, she didn't go to the police, she went to her cousin."

I open my hands and shake my head to make it clear that means nothing to me.

"Laura was one of the early adopters of post-Murder Files Tech Shifting. Her suit was paid for by her cousin, Dean Hollister."

Now this is beginning to make sense. Tech Shifting is still quite controversial to some. It involves having plugs inserted in your spine so you can wear metal animal suits. Everyone has their own reasons for doing it; for me it's a way to chill out after a hard week, using my black panther suit, Ink, to enter a different headspace for a while. A lot of the people at the local meets I arrange are the same. Some still can't let go of the memories of the original psychos who used the suits to enact some sick, blood-soaked werewolf fantasies, though. Dean Hollister is the man who created the gear and runs several successful businesses across the world. "What did he do?"

"Threatened them, mostly. In the end, they let her go with a severance package that would please most upper management level staff and let Mr. Hollister disentangle his companies from several bothersome contracts with them without having to pay the get-out fees. All Laura had to do was agree not to press charges. Ever since then, the younger Graves has been wary of Tech Shifters. He seems to think you might *all* have ties to Hollister."

I swallow hard. "Which means if I was the one to take a fake job there, I'd be safe."

"I...can't guarantee it. But it's likely. You fit the type of person he tends to have on his team too; female, aged eighteen to twenty-five, shorter than him. It makes sense. You fit aesthetically for him, but Ink would offer some protection. Maybe."

Damien coughs to get our attention and says, "This is all beginning to sound like one of my daughter's TV shows; all couples working through issues that haven't even come up yet. Look, what you're saying would potentially work, but you're missing something important here, Miss Tam. Say I went along with it. You haven't explained what's in it for me. I hate what this guy is doing, but I have a business to run.

"Frankly, what you're asking me to do is allocate resources away from our regular workload. That means time not being utilized against the daily struggles of keeping up to date, and expensive equipment being placed where it could get damaged. On top of that, Lori here, should she agree to doing this, is one of our best photographers, who I had planned to give a full week of work to after today. So, ignore my humanity—I'm certainly trying to—and give me something my money-making brain can work with."

Cassie nods. She looks thoughtful, though not surprised. "When it comes to time away from work, it wouldn't be. My plan is to make sure this stops entirely. Not only would copies of the footage be given to the police to facilitate an arrest, but I was thinking, as the press papers would allow it, you could legitimately use the footage. You could bill it as an undercover exposé of crime going unpunished, and the lengths ordinary people sometimes need to go to in order to ensure justice is served. So long as you place the blame on the company rather than the police, there won't be any legal ramifications. I would be happy to appear, and my client has already stated she might be able to sit down for a talk too.

"In terms of the equipment, you're right. I *was* hoping to use whatever you had to hand, as I figured you'd have some higher end stuff than I do. I do understand what you're saying, though. If anything gets damaged, bill me. I have a decent savings pot, and my client is also willing to field expenses if needed. And as to Lori's safety, I'll be monitoring it all. If something goes wrong, I'll be there to make sure Mr. Graves doesn't hurt anyone ever again."

Damien laughs. "Well, I wouldn't go as far as killing him. No offense, Lori. It does sound like you have a good handle on it all. I tell you what, I can check what we have that may work. And Lori, if you don't feel comfortable doing it, Joanne is a Tech Shifter too. I could give it to her as an assignment if needed. Or we could hire from the outside with Miss Tam's financial backing, of course."

I shake my head. "No. I'll do it. I'd rather it was me."

"Okay. Well, give me ten to grab some things, and we'll thrash it all out. I assume we're to start as soon as possible, so there's no sense in delaying it. You two talk, or whatever."

Damien leaves, and the second the door clicks shut. Cassie blurts, "I am so, so sorry. I wanted to tell you on the phone, but I was outside by my car so I could get moving quickly if the meeting was fine, and I didn't want anyone who shouldn't hear about it to hear about it, and..."

"Hey," I cut in, reaching out to grab her hand. "You're shaking."

"I know. I'm not normally...I just didn't want to put you on the spot. And now I have. I'm worried that's why you said yes, and I'm worried what will happen if you *do* do it."

"What happened to making sure he doesn't hurt anyone ever again? Cassie, I trust you to keep me as safe as you can. And I trust you to get there as quickly as you can if anything does happen."

"You're not scared at all?"

"I'm fucking terrified. But I was serious when I said I'd rather it was me. The Joanne Damien mentioned? She's only twenty and this is her first full-time job. On top of that, when you started talking about money, I couldn't help it. If you had as much saved up as you let on, you'd have higher-end equipment yourself. And what you do have goes toward paying your way through dry spells, right?"

"Not entirely." Cassie pulls her cell phone out and opens an app, then shows me the screen. It shows two bank accounts, one containing six thousand dollars, and the other fifty-three thousand, two hundred and seventy-nine dollars. "The smaller account I top up and use for general bills. I try to keep the balance healthy so I can get through the months that see less coming in without too much trouble."

"That's a lot in the larger one. Which begs the question, why don't you have more spy gear?"

"Spy gear?" She smiles, picking up on the only half-seriousness of my question. "It's not quite that. I use the account to pay the mortgage on my apartment. The monthly fee comes out, and I dip into it if I absolutely *need* something for a case. Mostly, I'm building it up with the bigger cases so I can pay the mortgage off in one go."

"Well, that's...sensible."

"You don't have to sound so shocked."

"I'm not, not really. I just had no idea you were doing it. How much is left to pay?"

"Around sixty thousand. So, I'm almost there."

I nod, rubbing my bottom lip between my thumb and index fingers. I never used to notice this little tic until Cassie pointed out I do it when I'm thinking about saying something, and I'm not sure how it'll come out. That's a perk of dating a detective who's borderline obsessed with noticing the small details that don't necessarily matter. "I know you said not to make a fuss for your birthday, but I have about twenty thousand in savings."

When Cassie replies, her tone is stern, but not unkind. "Don't you even think about it. I will not take a handout, *especially* from you."

"It won't be a handout; it'll be a birthday present."

"No, it won't be. I won't accept it, I'm sorry."

I sigh. "Okay, fair enough. It's a good thing I like your stubbornness. Most of the time."

A moment of silence passes. Eventually, Cassie says, "Even with the worry, I *am* glad you said yes. I trust you with this."

"So you should," Damien says, walking back in. "She's reliable, this one."

Chapter Two

I STRAIGHTEN THE collar on my blouse and pat a bit of lint off my work trousers. "Do I look the part?"

"You do," Cassie replies, rearranging the open windows on the laptop screen. She slowly moves the handbag on the passenger seat to another position and starts adjusting the individual window settings again. "Nervous?"

"Very. I mean, I've done undercover stuff before, sort of. When we found the files that led to the paid prison visit initiative? That was different. So long as we were careful, we weren't going to be targets. Plus, if we did screw up, it was just us who suffered. If things go wrong here, it could come back on Faye too."

Cassie stops what she's doing, slides out of her car, and places the borrowed laptop on her seat. She pulls me into a hug and then lightly places her hands on my shoulders. "You'll be fine. Faye knows what's going on, so she won't go out of her way to make it hard for you. She's going to keep her distance as much as possible, so Graves doesn't start making any moves to cut any perceived potential friendship. All you have to do is work."

"And make sure the cameras in the bag are facing the right way."

She nods. "Do you remember where they are?"

"The metal bobbles under the straps. Two in each side, one straight, one angled up."

"That's right, so make sure the straps are to the side, not resting over the front or back edge."

"No problem. I still think it looks weird on me, though. I don't normally carry bags this *chic*."

"Me neither."

I breathe in and release, giving the roof of Cassie's car a tap. "This is...three blocks away, right? If something *does* go wrong, how quickly can you get there?"

"I've been thinking about that. We need the distance so we don't arouse suspicion, but it does make it harder to rush in. So, I've been working on something." She pulls her cell phone out and unlocks the screen. "He should be here in a minute."

I smile and turn my head to the sky. Sure enough, a familiar shape is hurtling toward our place in the public parking lot behind the park. Cassie, spotting my reaction, smiles too and walks to the other side of the car. She opens the door and retrieves the bag. Within moments, a metal gargoyle lands on the roof of the car. He folds his wings and makes a slow turn to Cassie.

"Caw."

"Hi, Bert," she says. "You see Lori?"

Bert turns toward me, and the metal sheets around his eyes pull apart slightly. "Caw," he confirms.

"Lori is helping us with a case, and it's possibly going to be a bit dangerous. Can you get a lock on her, please?"

Bert waddles across the roof of the car and squats in front of me. His eyes flash a few times before switching to a solid red again. He lets out a metallic *chirrup*.

"Good. I'm going to give you a location, and I want you to stick there all the time Lori is there. Follow her but keep hidden. If she's in trouble, get in there. Intimidation only."

"Caw."

"I'm serious, Bert. As much as I'd love to see what you could do with the person we're going after, we can't have injuries on this one. Intimidation only. Understand?"

Bert slowly opens his beak, the *ahh* joining the scraping metal to create an almost-sigh. "Caw."

"You'll keep me safe, won't you?" I say and give him a stroke. The more I interact with him, the less I view him as a machine. Even so, the metal he's made of is—necessarily—solid. It's far harder than the flexible compound my Ink suit is made of. It makes it difficult not to acknowledge that he *is* mechanical. Ink is pliable enough to feel like an extension of *me*, but Bert is a solid mass of metal. I *am* happy to see him, though.

Bert nods his head, nudging my hand with his beak, and Cassie says, "He's really taken to you, hasn't he?"

"He has. I'm still not certain about having him meet Ink yet. He's lovely, but I don't fancy shocking him." Cassie nods in agreement and the sun catches the design on her tie. She tends to wear tidy black ones, with various animals printed on them. The animals are also in black, so unless you're looking, you wouldn't notice. I squint and ask, "Is that a panther?"

Cassie follows my eyeline and nods. "Yeah. It felt fitting, given we're working together on this one."

"You're too superstitious with this stuff for that to be the only reason. What do panthers symbolize?"

"They weren't very common in China, but you're right, we did apply a meaning to them. One on its own represents the taming of cruelty."

"That *is* fitting. You keep wearing it throughout the case, and hopefully, it'll work its magic."

Cassie nods in agreement and checks the time on her phone. "Okay. Well, your first day is due to start in twenty minutes. You'll be a new face in his territory, which may make him wary. I doubt he'll do anything today at all. Be careful, though."

"Sure." I grab the bag and give Cassie another hug. We both breathe each other in and then part, me to my car and she to the front seat of hers.

WHEN I REACH the front of the building, the barrier is up. It's one of those raised-out-of-the-floor chunks of metal that can really damage a car if you ignore it. There's a security guard waiting in a little hut to monitor visitors. He leans out from behind the glass and asks, "Name?"

"Lori Redwood. It's my first day, I'm...oh, hang on." I reach into the handbag and pull out the temporary work pass I've been sent and hand it over to the guard. "Workload delivery and complaints handling."

The man nods and hands the card back. "Tuesday is an odd day to start; they usually go for a Monday. Still, welcome aboard. The staff parking is right behind the building. I doubt you'll have an assigned spot yet, so head to one with a green-tipped bollard at the back, those are the guest ones. After that, the main desk will take you up. Oh, and don't worry about the gathering out the front. They're filming a documentary for NHNS."

I smile sweetly. "Sounds exciting."

"Yeah, they already spoke to me but said they might come back again later. Barrier's down, head on in."

I wave a thanks and drive in, watching my colleagues from the office as they ask some guy in a suit whatever questions they've come up with. It's taken four days to get this set up, thanks in part to natural delays being caused by the weekend being non-working days for Fast Ship Limited. Damien was able to convince Mr. Graves Sr. to let us in easily enough, all he had to do was turn on the charm a little and make it sound like we *might* be in the market for a partnership if all goes well. Discounted rates for us, and free advertising for them, that sort of thing. It was all nonsense, of course, but it worked.

The problem was the nature of what we're doing means we needed confidentiality, even with our fellow workers. So, Damien is the one doing the interviews, and one of our newer video guys is holding the camera. I've not really met him, which is important as we don't want him to give the game away. He won't know our real agenda regardless. The press passes allow them both on site for the day. The plan, if everything played out how Damien wanted, was for him to tell security that one of his party was off sick and to spring the job on the cameraman at the last minute even though his press pass was already set.

My pass has *accidentally* been set to allow a full four days of filming. That gives me some leeway, but it's still time limited, so I need to make sure I blend in quickly enough for the younger Graves to start acting like he would normally.

I find one of the guest parking spaces relatively easily and head back around the front of the building, being careful to keep my head down as I pass the interview going on, just in case. The receptionist takes my card, and within moments, we're starting a silent elevator ride to the third floor.

"I DIDN'T REQUEST any further staff," Mr. Graves grunts down his phone, his eyes wandering over me. "Right. So, what? One month slightly below targets and we're under efficiency measures? It. Was. A. Blip."

Normally, if I found myself in this sort of situation, I'd be doing my best to appear unassuming. It really doesn't take much pretending in this case. Lewis Graves is not the biggest man I've ever met, far from it, but even now, while he's clearly holding back, he's got a natural aggression to him. The designer stubble and over-gelled hair work wonders to harden his face, which adds to the effect.

"Fine. You still could have told me in advance," he says and chucks the phone back onto the receiver. He rises to his feet and walks out of his mini office, giving me a gruff "This way" as he passes.

Once we're out on the main floor, he uses a loud series of claps to grab everyone's attention. The sound of typing dies down, and all eyes are on us as he says, "Turns out we're not trusted to keep on top of things. Not by HR and stat management, in any case. This is..." He clicks his fingers at me.

"Lori," I reply.

"Lori," he repeats. "She's joining us, starting today. Gabby."

A lady at the back of the room stands up. "Yes?"

"You're smack in the middle of productivity, but you've been here the longest, so she's *your* problem. She's set up on the spare desk apparently. Show her what to do. Faye, you're working at fifty percent efficiency, so *this* is on you. See if you can guess what we'll be discussing at your weekly performance review. Now, get back to work."

And with that he heads off to his mini office. He makes a point of slamming the door as he enters. Gabby walks over and offers me a handshake I gladly take. She looks like every stereotypical office woman I've ever read about; tidy ponytail, plain office wear, and subtle makeup that would look good on an ad campaign at a university. She's pretty much the poster girl for 'you have a future here.'

I glance back toward the recently slammed door and try, "He seems...nice?"

"Sometimes," she replies. "Come on, I'll get you set up. Did they give you a temp card?" I nod and pull it out of my pocket. "Good, you'll need it to log in. Security being what it is, you should probably have the card on show. I might have a spare lanyard if you need one?"

"That would be great, thanks."

She pulls out a card reader from behind the monitor and, after checking it's plugged in, shows me how to switch the machine on and get everything open. Our friend in HR has set up some cloned and altered files for me to work on so I don't get into trouble under confidentiality laws. They must look legit as Gabby doesn't seem to notice at all. And so, the first couple of hours of my day are spent going over shortcut keys and the correct path to take through the system. Finally, we hit lunchtime and the staggered breaks start rolling out.

"You can all go one at a time," Mr. Graves tells us, "to make sure we don't drop any more productivity."

So, I find myself sitting alone in a small rest area that's essentially a converted meeting room. Even before the addition of the fridge and sink, I doubt they would have fit more than four people in here comfortably. The advantage to this is I can start reviewing videos on my phone. The cameras are streaming to Cassie in real time but also uploading to a shared system every couple of minutes, so I can get a good idea of what we're capturing. I've already moved the bag a few times, trying a few things out.

The desk he has me at makes it difficult to catch anything that happens at Faye's desk I might get some snatches of it, but it's not ideal. Anything happening in his office is almost out my line of sight too, unless I get the bag up on the in tray. Good job they aren't entirely paperless. Even then it'll be difficult to catch anything if the lady directly opposite me stands up.

My allotted half hour goes quickly, and the potential shot blocker enters the room. "Hi," she says. "Lori, wasn't it?"

"Yeah," I say. "Sorry, I think I missed your name?"

"It's Jo. And don't worry about it, the first few days can be a bit overwhelming. Anyway, time's up."

I return her smile and sweep the crumbs from my sandwich into the little plastic bin by the table. She takes a seat in the corner, and I return to my desk for another few hours of tedium. The one bright spot was when Mr. Graves was called to go and speak to the interview team. They didn't come into the office itself. I don't know whether that was at his request or Damien's, but the idea of him talking himself up made me smile. Faye's body language has made it clear how worn down she is, and the moment he left, she was able to relax a little. Even if I didn't know what she was going through, *everyone* here is walking on eggshells around him. The more he tries to make himself look like a great boss, the bigger the fall he's going to have.

THE END OF the day comes around and I notice Faye leaves silently on her own while the other girls mill around and say a few pleasant goodbyes to one another. If I wasn't doing what I was, I may not even have noticed how odd it was that the team was all female other than Graves himself. Even in a team of six—seven including me—you'd expect a mix unless there was a good reason for it not to be.

I think better of mentioning either observation yet in case it screws everything up. Instead, I give my thanks to everyone and leave with Gabby and Jo who are, to their credit, doing their best to make me feel welcome.

"Tomorrow," Jo promises, "we'll get to know each other better. Especially that."

I notice she's pointing to my head plugs. Sounds like I'll be getting interrogated tomorrow. *Great.*

I make it back to my car and, after sitting down and taking a moment to compose myself, I grab my phone and dial Cassie. She picks up quickly, but only gets as far as, "Hey," before my attention is drawn to a knocking on the window.

I look up and, seeing who's there, reply, "I'll call you back. My boss wants a chat."

I hang up, place the phone in its holder on the dashboard, and lower the window. Graves ducks down a little so he can rest an arm across the hole housing the glass. "Hey, so you know, I checked some of your work. It all seems fine so far, but you're a bit on the slow side, yeah?"

"Oh, sorry," I try. "It's just all really new to me, ya know?"

"Yeah, yeah," he replies. "I get it. Just make sure you learn how best to spend your time. You seem to be getting on well with everyone, but don't let it descend into more chat than work."

"Okay," I say, trying to make myself seem as small as possible.

The silence is accompanied by him giving me an arrogant smile. Finally, he stands up, knocks the roof of my car, and says, "See you tomorrow."

I notice he takes a few steps back but doesn't leave, so make the decision to do so myself. He's like a lion driving someone out of his territory, and I don't want to trigger an urge in him to hunt me down. I pull away, making sure to keep my eyes averted, and say, "Phone, call Cassie Tam, speaker phone mode on."

We barely make it through a whole ring before Cassie picks up. "Lori? You okay?"

"Yeah. Yeah, I'm fine. He wanted to tell me how slow I am, and to make sure I don't start chatting more than working."

"He's trying to isolate you a little."

"Sounds like it. I'm hoping it's just him asserting himself early on. He was making it *really* clear he was the boss."

"*Diu.* Do you want Bert to be on high alert? Or to follow you home?"

"I'm tempted, but no. I don't think he'll pursue me, not right now. Tomorrow, I'll be extra careful. How are the angles on the videos looking to you?"

"Mixed," she concedes. "As far as I know, he's done things on the main floor, in his office, and in the rest area. Right now, the main office is patchy, but you may catch something. His office is almost a dead end. And the rest area...if it's just one of you at a time in there, I guess that's out too."

"I don't think it'll stay that way. He was pretty pissed about having a new staff member due to failing productivity. Give it a day or two and I think we'll be looking at multiple people at once. Did Faye mention anything about how her relationship with her co-workers is?"

Cassie pauses. "She said it used to be good until she became a target. He'd apparently been picking on another girl, Jo. When she said something to him about how inappropriate it was to be yelling at staff, he switched his focus to her, and they all distanced themselves."

"I was getting that impression. How does she feel about it all?"

"She's...not happy. But she understands. A few people warned her not to get involved."

"I can see why. He didn't even do anything to her today, but she was still so...she was hurting."

"Well, that's what we're trying to stop. How are you coping so far?"

I sigh. "Our bonus meeting at the end was a little scary. So far, I'm okay."

"Okay. Good. Listen, I need to really go over these videos and see what the best angles are going to be. Did you want me to come over and we can work at it together?"

I smile. "Honestly? Part of me does, but I *do* have to get some things done tonight. I need to fill in some audits for the Tech Shift Meets. Besides, I know you don't *need* me to be there when you do it. You're just worried about me. It's sweet."

She laughs then, and it's nervous, but genuine. "I'm that transparent, eh?"

"To me you are. Most of the time. I kept the rotations in a sequence anyway. Equal movements each time. Tell me which one you want in each position; like third angle next to me, second on the riser, and stuff. I'll work with that."

"Okay, I can do that. But are you sure?"

"Yeah. Right now, you'll be worrying whatever we do. If you're there with me, you'll just make a fuss and we'll both end up not doing what we're meant to be doing. For me, it's not a big deal. For Faye? Not so much."

"I'm a little more professional than that, you know."

"You also care more than you let on. Or am I wrong?"

She pauses again, a little longer this time. "There's no right answer to that, is there?"

"There's an honest one."

Another pause. "Okay, I'll go over this lot back at the apartment. Any trouble, you call me."

I smile and shake my head. One day, she'll open up a bit more. "Sure. Goodnight, Cassie."

"Goodnight."

MY SECOND DAY in the office started with an early morning meeting. Mr. Graves was relatively calm throughout and kept things brief. Stats were stable but needed to improve, and weekly one-to-one meetings would begin today. I would be excused due to only being there for one day. After that, he returned to his office to arrange his records for said meetings and left us to our work.

After Gabby was called away for her one-to-one, Jo took the opportunity to lean around her monitor and ask, "How are you finding things so far?"

"It's okay. Fairly mind-numbing, but the system is intuitive at least."

She nods and moves her face back to her own screen but continues talking as she types. "What did you do before you came here?"

Mixing the truth with fiction is the best way to keep up the pretense, so I reply, "Freelance stuff, mostly. I was doing some formatting work for a couple of news sites, took a few phone calls, that sort of thing. So not too different, really. All uncredited, other than my bank account, of course."

"It must have been pretty interesting at times. I mean, did you ever get to see any big stories before they dropped?"

"A couple, but nothing that wasn't already out there elsewhere. It's the reporters and photographers who get to see the stuff really early."

"So, what made you leave?"

"Inconsistency in work levels. When you're freelance, you get paid per job, so if there was a dry spell, I'd be living off my emergency funds. This is similar enough to fit my experience, different enough to not send me to asleep yet, but regular enough to be worthwhile. What about you? Why'd you join up?"

"I used to work part time in a café, but really, I wanted something with a little more opportunity for upward mobility. When I saw this job advertised, I figured it was a good bet and went for it."

"Are you looking to move upward soon? Maybe to Mr. Graves's level?"

She stops typing then and leans around the monitor again. When she replies, she keeps her voice low. "Seriously, don't even joke about that." She leans back and continues, "Not yet. Really, the best way to move up *here* is to move sideways first, I think. You just have to wait for the right opportunity. You joining up could actually help a few of the girls."

I note the emphasis she put on "here" and cross my fingers that the camera caught it. "Oh?"

"We've had a pretty consistent number of staff on the team, and I doubt Graves'll want the increase to be permanent. Spending time training you to shift you off again seems like a waste, right? So, it's gotta be one of us who moves on."

"So what you're saying is I'm stuck here."

"That's about the size of it. Sorry. Work's not the best subject for a chat, though. You got anything going on in the real world? Seeing anyone?"

I hesitate. I wouldn't feel comfortable lying entirely, but how much can I get away with saying here?

"That's a yes," Jo says. "Come on, tell me about him. I want to know if he's worth stealing."

"She, actually. And hands off."

Jo laughs. "No problem there. How did the two of you meet?"

"I needed some help with an issue at home and she came around and fixed it all."

"What, was it a DIY job? Or a tech issue, maybe?"

"Something like that. She ended up not charging me if I agreed to go on a date with her. I kinda had my eye on her from early on in the job, so I said yes."

"That's sweet. How long have you been together?"

"About three and a half months now." *Which puts her halfway to the point where people normally walk away from you, so let's try not to blow it.*

Gabby walks out of Mr. Graves's office and walks back around my side of the desk. "Jo, you're up. He seems okay at the moment."

"Okay, good," she replies, locking her screen. "That's something. Lori here was just telling me about her girlfriend."

And with that she's off across the room. She's trying to remain calm, but her steps are faltering. It's a little different to how she's come across so far. I guess she was masking.

"I did wonder," Gabby says. I turn and give her an odd look and she clarifies, "If you were single. You're a lot less stern looking than the couple of Tech Shifters I've met before, so it seemed like you'd probably be seeing someone. Tech Shifting can put people off, right?"

"It can. A lot of the Tech Shifters I know are single. It still leaves a bad taste in people's mouths ever since the Murder Files. The misinformation the sensationalist end of the press throws out doesn't help either. Not everyone is doomed to loneliness, though. Sure, it can get a bit much for a lot of people, but sometimes you find someone who accepts you for you even if they aren't sure to begin with."

"Is that what happened with your partner?"

"I like to think so. She's a little nervous of us, but she really wants to get through her hang-ups. That's important."

"She's nervous. Makes sense. I mean, it *is* all a bit weird, isn't it?"

"Gee, thanks."

"I'm joking, I'm joking," Gabby replies. "Don't forget to follow the time tracking to make sure the team isn't being given too much, by the way."

"Ah, yeah. Thanks."

"Seriously, though, I *do* see why people would be put off dating a Tech Shifter. The general public perception isn't great. Even the police team are viewed as scary more than anything, right?"

"They are, yeah. For good reason too."

"Okay, so here's one. And tell me if I'm prying too much here, but why don't you see many Tech Shifter couples? You know, where both people are Shifters?"

I finish what I'm typing and turn to face Gabby. "That depends where you go. Most people who get into it do so because they enjoy roleplay. If you're just doing it for fun, and yes, some do, you're more likely to end up with another Tech Shifter."

"This ties into the F groups, doesn't it? What were they?"

"Furries and Fetishists. The third one, Freaks, don't tend to get through the screening process anymore. The ones I just mentioned, doing it for fun, are usually First F's, Furries. But there aren't as many Furs in New Hopeland. Most of us are Second F's."

"Fetishists."

"Exactly. Look at it as a spin-off from pet-play." I notice Gabby's blank expression and clarify, "We roleplay as animals as a form of escapism. It lets us get away from problems in the real world and be something that doesn't have to deal with the day-to-day stresses."

"Oh. Right. I mean, okay, you can see why people would think it's a bit odd, right?"

I shake my head. "Not really. Some people de-stress with a drink, or music, or visiting somewhere they find relaxing. Me, I pretend I'm a panther. Different path, same end result."

Gabby opens her mouth to respond, but stops, shakes her head, and instead asks, "So, why does that mean you'd be less likely to end up with another Tech Shifter?"

"Me personally? It doesn't. Being with my partner, who isn't a Tech Shifter, means I'm not going to. I think what it comes down to for some is, even with it not being a sexual thing for most Second F's, it is still a submissive headspace for many. If you're naturally submissive, you *may* be more interested in a more dominant partner. Depending how much focus you put on the roles in terms of your needs, of course. So, if Tech Shifting is submissive in nature, you're more likely to view other Shifters as sub too. I mean, if one or more of you is switch, that could work, I suppose."

"What's switch?"

I smile. "I'll let you look it up yourself. But do it at home. Would you like to know the biggest reason you don't see as many Tech Shift couples in New Hopeland?"

"Sure."

"It's because we're all so different. You can't base a relationship on just one shared interest."

The door to Mr. Graves's office opens, and Jo walks out. She heads straight for Faye, places a hand on her shoulder, and sends her on her way. I watch Faye shuffle toward her meeting and, once the door is closed, lean around to Jo and ask, "Is she okay? What was her name...Faye, isn't it?"

A worried look passes between Jo and Gabby, and Jo sighs. "I suppose you'll see what's going on soon enough. Mr. Graves isn't particularly nice to her."

"Really? I mean, he seemed a little, I don't know, aggressive? Not really more than most managers I've met, though."

"What you got from him is what most of us get," Gabby replies. "As for Faye... She's his chosen victim right now."

"Victim?"

"He picks someone and focuses on them. They essentially become the target for all his frustrations."

"It used to be me," Jo whispers. "He never went too far; he was just really critical, you know?"

"About your work?"

"Work, makeup, clothes, the way I stack papers, what I was eating. If he could criticize it, he would. Faye stood up for me, and he switched to her. I still feel shitty about that, but what can I do? If I say anything, he'll start on me again. And he's been going further with her. I don't think I could handle that."

"Careful," Gabby cuts in, and Jo stops talking.

I turn to Gabby, subtly nudging the bag around a little so the camera is facing her, and ask, "Why does he do it?"

"Because he's living in the past." She sighs. "He was passed over for promotion years ago, or so I was told. It was the first time he'd gone for it, and the other person was pretty similar to him in terms of experience. The only real difference was she was female, and he was male. So, he zoned in on that. Once he moved to this place, he kinda decided no woman was ever going to be more powerful than him again."

"That's ridiculous," I reply.

"It is, if it's true. But he definitely doesn't like women being on the same or a higher rung than him. Once, before he got his first middle management job, he was given a one-to-one trainer to work with. You know, show him the ropes like I've been doing with you? Well, he wouldn't listen to her. She was off for a week, they gave him a male trainer, and all of a sudden, he started learning. The moment she came back, he dropped again. He even stopped doing the things the guy had told him just because it was a woman telling him to do them now. She challenged him on it, and he followed her into the elevator. I don't know what he said to her in there, but when they came out again, she was in tears."

"Didn't she report him?"

"Of course she did. But when your dad owns the business and thinks you're a poor, mistreated little darling who's tragically misunderstood, you can get away with *a lot*. She left shortly after."

"Which probably cemented the idea he had power in his head."

"Exactly. And the higher he goes in the company the worse he gets. I've been on his team three times now, so I've seen what he's…"

The door to Mr. Graves's office opens and Faye walks out, her slumped body language making her look thoroughly deflated.

"At least he didn't shout at her this time," Jo whispers, and we all get back to work.

"I REALLY WANT TO talk to her," I say, handing Cassie a mug. "But I know I can't, or we'd risk giving the game away."

"There's always the possibility he'd become wary too if it looks like she may have a new ally, especially one he's not as likely to want to mess with. He hasn't tried anything else with you, has he?"

"No. If he wanted to, I think he would have. You couldn't see it on the video, but Faye's body language when she came out his office was…he didn't shout at her, we'd have heard that, and she didn't have any visible new marks, so he didn't hit her. But he said *something*."

Cassie places her hand on my arm, her eyes full of concern. "Are you sure you're okay to continue with this?"

"Definitely," I reply, my voice resolute. "Especially after today. It's not like I didn't believe what you told us, but when you're in the middle of it, even at the low end, it rams home what's happening."

We sit on the couch and I continue, "Honestly, I thought there were supposed to be laws in place to stop people acting like this."

"There are. When you've done investigative stuff, you must have seen people bending the rules, though. Especially those in power. The more control you have, the more you seek. That's what it looks like to me, anyway."

"Even so, this is so blatant, and everyone seems to know about it. It's bullying, and it's misogyny. Dad at the top or not, I really don't know how he gets away with it."

"Lewis Graves is part of a dying breed. You see them once in a while when you're a PI, usually in spousal disputes, but not as much as you would have fifty years ago. They act the way they do because, for whatever reason, they need to feel tough. They need to feel powerful. And to do that, they figure out who they *think* is below them and kick down. The truth is, even in the absolute cesspits of society, the holes full of cold-blooded killers and organized crime syndicates, there are so many people with much more legitimate power than them. If someone like him had to deal with someone like that, they wouldn't last a minute, even if it never went beyond verbal sparring.

"And that's the thing. Deep down, people like Lewis Graves *know* they're weak. They know they're nothing more than bullies, scrambling and crawling over the people they try to bury. That's how he gets away with it. He's desperate. And desperation makes you cling on tight and take every shortcut you can find."

"And do the desperate bullies always fall in the end?"

Cassie looks at me, studying my face. Her expression is enough to give me my answer. Being who she is, she decides not to try comforting me with lies. "No, they don't. Sometimes, the bad guys win. All any of us can do is try to make sure it doesn't happen often."

Chapter Three

"I DID?" FAYE asks, her eyes darting away from her screen to Mr. Graves's office door. His silhouette is visible behind the partially frosted glass, and he has his body angled toward her. The ring tone meant it was an internal call. "No, no, I didn't notice."

She goes quiet for a moment, nodding and giving a simple audible response, then wipes her brow. "No, sorry, I understand. I can fix it, just give me a minute...you did?"

We all sense the tension rise, and Jo starts glancing over her shoulder at her colleague. Faye drops her head into one hand and says, "You didn't need to tell him, I could have...no, no, I understand. Thank you. I'll get right on it."

The sound of the telephone being placed on the receiver silences not only the call but the whole room. It also gives Mr. Graves his cue to leave his office, his face red. His expression is enough to prompt me to nudge my bag to the side, trying to get it at the best angle to catch what happens as he storms over and asks Faye, "Do you know what I just received?"

"An e-mail," she replies.

"Say that again, so I can actually hear you," he snaps.

"An e-mail," she repeats.

"And what did the e-mail say?"

"I messed up the time allocation for acquisitions department three. But the Shaws are twins, and they have the same first initial, so..."

"Is that an excuse?" he cuts in. "Do you remember what I told you about excuses?"

"They...they don't change the fact of the actions that need excusing."

"Thus?"

"Thus, rendering them worthless."

Mr. Graves leans in, placing one hand on the back of Faye's chair and the other on the desk next to her. With her sitting in the corner of the room, he's effectively blocking her in with no way to escape what I'm guessing is a thoroughly terrifying look. "Which is exactly what your work is like right now. I could ignore a little inconsistency in quality if you put out what I expected, but the fact is you don't. Were you aware you have the lowest productivity in the team?"

"N-no."

"Well, you do. And you know what that means, don't you? You're doing less fucking work than the new girl." He turns and clicks his fingers at me, and I struggle not to respond. "You. Lori. Stand up."

I do as I'm told, and he asks me, "Tell me, as a new member of staff, do you think it is acceptable for an experienced member of staff to be underperforming against someone who hasn't even finished their third day yet?"

I swallow hard and reply, "In fairness, I *am* working easier jobs at the moment. Or that's what I was told, anyway. My caseload is being kept basic while I learn the systems."

"I did not ask for chapter and verse. It is a simple yes or no question."

I let my shoulders sag. There's no way to lessen what he's doing here. "No."

"And since you clearly like talking, what *would* you expect to happen when comparing the stats of staff members?"

I wince, knowing what I'm expected to say. "I would expect experienced staff to be capable of outperforming new starters, at least until they're trained up sufficiently to perform at their best."

"Sit down," he commands, and I do so. He turns back to Faye, who is now sobbing quietly in her chair. He curls his lip in disgust. "Look at you. You're a mess. Go and clean yourself up, then come back and fix the issues you've caused for acquisitions."

Mr. Graves storms back to his office, and the second his door closes, Faye gets up and bolts toward the bathroom. I start to stand up to follow her, but Gabby is already there to place a hand on my shoulder and say, "I wouldn't."

"Someone has to do *something*," I say.

"They have before. Faye did. Look at her now. Listen, Lori, it's a fucking awful thing to say, but you have an advantage right now. Don't screw that up."

"An advantage, huh? And what's that?"

"These," she says, tapping on my head plugs. I hold back on snapping about how much I hate when people do that, and she continues, "I told you before, I've been in his team three times now. He keeps me around because I do what I'm told, and I work hard enough to be useful to his precious stats. That's how most people cope with him. You bide your time and behave yourself until you can take a sideways transfer. You, though, you're similar enough to the one person who got the better of him that he'll leave you be if you play ball."

"Similar to her how? Because I'm a Tech Shifter?"

"Exactly."

"It's not right," I retort.

"No, it's not. But look around you. Every single person on this team is female, aged eighteen to twenty-five. Me, at thirty, I'm too old for him to focus on now, so I can relax a little. The rest of you all need to find some way to avoid being the next Faye. You have that already."

"Don't you feel any shame for not trying to stop this? If you're too old for him to be interested in picking on, maybe you could say something?"

She shakes her head. "I'm a coward, Lori. I know I am. I had a chance to say something the first time he did this, but I didn't. Do you know why? Because I was scared if I spoke up and he still got away with it, I'd be next. I've had chances to leave his team since then, but I just keep going with him. This right now, explaining it all to you? *This* is all I can do. Try to help new starters so they're less likely to become victims. It's my penance for being a coward. Sometimes, someone doesn't listen. Like Faye. And *that's* what happens."

I SIT BACK in my car seat, ignoring the other people pulling into the public parking lot a few blocks from Main Street. "I wanted to tell her she's wrong, you know? But I couldn't. I know I need to stay silent, because we want to catch him on camera, but I *could* try taking him on and making myself a target."

"Lori," Cassie says, her voice wavering slightly down the phone. "You..."

"I know, I know. Doing that would risk him starting the process over with me, and I only have one more day's worth of filming on the press pass. But the thing is, even if I had all the time in the world, I know I couldn't do it. Not really. I'm pissed at Gabby for being a coward, but the truth is, I'm just as bad, because I couldn't knowingly put myself in that position. It's like...at home, it's *my* territory to protect. You *have* to do that, whichever way you can even if you think you can't. In there, though? I want to react, and I tell myself I can't because we need the footage, but even if I wasn't filming him, the truth is I still wouldn't be able to. I'd be exactly like the rest of them, and that just...it really sucks."

"Lori, it's okay. You're not a coward. What you're saying, damn near anyone would be exactly the same. But the fact is, you *are* doing something right now. The footage you got today is good. And the stuff the other staff were saying? I double checked, and the press passes mean you can speak to anyone and film it. If they weren't informed, that's HR's fault, so it'll still stand up when we pass it on to the PD. I think...I think you can probably step away now."

I wipe the tears from my eyes, knowing full well what the answer to my next question is going to be. "Tell me honestly, Cassie. Is what we got today enough to *guarantee* action?"

Cassie inhales sharply. "Not a criminal conviction, no. But it will probably mean he gets fired. Even with his dad running things, if it's going to hit the press, he'll need to be seen to be acting on it."

"Then he'll still be out there, ready to lash out at everyone who said something on camera. No. I can't take the abuse for her, but I can still help Faye. I'll keep going until we either have what we need, or we run out of time. Whichever comes first."

"Are you sure?"

"Yeah. Yeah, I'm sure."

"Then...let's try to force it. I have an idea. I'll speak to Faye, and if she's willing, then...tomorrow should be over quickly, at least. Do you want me to come over and we can talk it all through?"

"No. No, I'm tired. Really tired. Just let me know what you have in mind before tomorrow, okay? I'm going to go home and get some dinner, then go to bed."

"Okay. And Lori? I'm proud of you."

I have no suitable response, so I hang up and try to calm myself. When sitting here dwelling on things doesn't work, I rub my eyes and mumble, "Okay, Lori. You've had days like this before. Driving isn't going to be your friend right now, and you're too far away to walk. You need something difficult to focus your mind. Birthday shopping. That'll do it."

Cassie's birthday is only a few days away now and I still haven't bought her anything. I doubt she'd mind even without all of this going on, but I want to do *something* at least. I just don't know what.

So, I lock up the car and take a walk up Main Street. The issue becomes clear really quickly; for all the shops we have here, I have no clue what the best present would be to get her. It's while I'm idly browsing the window of a VOD film distributor that I catch sight of the reflection of someone walking by. I turn my head slowly to watch him walking away and make a snap decision to run and catch up.

"Excuse me," I say, coming up beside him. When he ignores me, I step in front of him and stop, causing him to do the same. I look him up and down, making sure I've not made a mistake. His is a face that is rarely shown on the news, but one everyone seems to know. At least if you know people like Cassie. "You're Devin Carmichael."

He crosses his arms and tilts his head to give me an irritated glare from under his cowboy hat. When he speaks, his accent is thick, and carries with it an annoyed tone. "And you're Lori Redwood. Look, what happened to your brother? That was business. I already told Caz, I ain't discussing it any further than that. I thought she'd dropped this already."

I flinch at the mention of his part in my brother's death, but his last sentence pulls me back quickly. "Wait. Dropped what?"

He frowns. "You didn't know?"

"Know what?"

"Ah, shit." He rubs his stubble and starts staring off toward an alley, then adds, "Come with me," and starts walking up the street again.

DEVIN RETURNS TO our seat and places a cup of green tea in front of me. He sits down opposite me, takes a mouthful of what looks like whiskey, and nods to my cup. "You look run down. Trust me, that'll perk you up a bit. It's *just* green tea, but it works wonders, I find."

I take a careful sip, but it's far too hot to drink right now, so I place the cup back down and take in our surroundings. "I've never seen this place before."

He shrugs. "Alleyway cafés. There are a few in the city, but they're all pretty outta the way. Unless you walk in the right circles, you're not likely to come across them. Ya saw there were no signs outside, right?"

"Yeah. I did notice that."

"The advantage of places like this is they all know me well enough to give me and any guest I bring along a private booth. I figured you'd appreciate some quiet."

"I guess. So, what's Caz been up to?"

He leans back and smiles, his teeth the most visible thing under the hat he's showing no interest in taking off. "She's probably gonna kill me for this. Verbally, at least. She's inquired a few times as to whether I'd be interested in stopping by and talking to you about the business with Eddie. She seemed to think it would all help give you some closure, or something. I told her it was a dumb idea."

"It isn't one of her best," I concede.

"The last she mentioned it, she said she'd figured out how stupid it was. That was way back when she was looking for that Tech Shift performer Kitsune's lost dog, so when you came running up, I figured maybe she'd gotten back onto it."

"No. She never mentioned it all. That was probably smarter than the idea itself."

"Uh-huh. So, if you weren't looking to ask me questions you weren't gonna like the answers to, why *did* you stop me in the middle of the street?"

I try the tea again. Devin was right, it does seem to be helping now I can get a proper mouthful. "You've known Cassie a long time, right?"

"More than most, I suppose. Met her on one of her early cases here. Though she already had a reputation back in Vancouver by then, so I knew who she was before that."

"She did?"

"Don't sound so surprised. I do work outside New Hopeland when the right job comes up. And certain people attract the attention of certain other people. In this case, people I happen to have close ties to. Don't worry. She may not know she gets tongues wagging, but it's all good things they say. Caz is stubborn, but she's fair."

"That sounds about right. It's, um…it's her birthday this Saturday. She's twenty-eight."

"Okay. And? This ain't gonna be some surprise party invite, is it?"

"No, nothing like that. It's just—I want to get her something she'll really love, and I don't have a clue where to begin."

"Hmm. I guess flowers wouldn't really be her thing, would they?"

"See, I think she'd appreciate it if I *did* do something like that, but she wouldn't *love* it. Cassie is sweet, and kind, and tough, and smart, but…she's practical more than anything. I keep coming back to that. She only buys things for herself when she needs them. So, I thought maybe, given what *you* do, you may be able to recommend something she'd be able to use for work? Like something she's unlikely to have but likely to need?"

When he doesn't respond immediately, I add, "I really don't like you. Honestly, after what happened, I don't think I ever will. But I'm desperate here."

Devin studies my face for a moment, then laughs. "Jeez, you aren't kidding. You must be *really* desperate if you're coming to *me* for that. She's really got her claws in you, ain't she? Okay. Okay, let's see." He raises his glass but stops short of drinking anything. Instead, he smiles again and places it back on the table. "I wonder."

"What?"

"Now, I've been involved indirectly with a number of Caz's cases, some of which she doesn't know about. I've bailed her out here and there. Not with what she's been doing, you understand. More with the less savory people who take notice. But there have been a few times I've seen her working on things where a certain tool would have sped things up for her. She's clearly never bought one, likely due to the prices they charge around here. It just so happens I may be able to get you a damn good deal on one."

"Okay, so what is it?"

"It's a little thing called a ping box. Now, the best place to go would be Joe Farrah's gun shop. You know where it is?" I nod. "Joe's a close personal friend of mine. He ain't so sold on Caz, so you'd do well not to mention her, at least not right away. Thing is, he *will* try to charge you well above what he should for one of these things. If he gives you a price above forty dollars, you tell him I sent you, and I still have the photo from back in Kansas."

"That sounds shady."

"Not as much as you'd think. He messed me around a little last week, though, so it's good to remind him I *do* have some leverage."

"Ping box. Joe Farrah. Kansas photo. Okay. Thank you."

"Don't mention it," he says, and downs his drink. He stands up and says, "You can finish your drink in peace here. Joe will be open for business for a few hours yet, and if not, he'll be there tomorrow."

"WELL, FUCK YOU too, Sammy," a voice yells from somewhere inside the store.

"It's Alex," another man yells back, storming out through the door. He notices me waiting to go in and says loud enough to make sure whoever's inside hears it, "I wouldn't go in there if I were you, lady. The gear's overpriced, and I reckon half of it's stolen."

"That's it," comes the first voice again, and a man with an excruciatingly bad receding hairline and ponytail combo storms out. "Get off my property. Go on. Ignore him, Miss, he's an ex-employee with no regard for the rules. Didn't like his wages being withheld, that's all."

"It was one box of bullets, Joe," Alex says as I walk by.

"One box, my ass," Joe says, guiding me inside. "And even if it was, theft is theft."

"No, no, I totally understand," I say, trying to avoid getting too caught up in it all.

Joe moves behind the counter and opens his arms to the shelves. "So, what are you in the market for? Looking at you, I'm gonna guess it's one of the new TS upgrades, right? You full animal or one of them humanoid things?"

"Animal, but that's not what I'm after. I was actually looking for a ping box. Do you have one?"

"Of course I've got a ping box," he replies and starts rummaging under the desk. "They don't sell often, but they're useful things. I only stock the one type, though. Top of the line, New Hopeland made, and all that. So, what? You think someone's watching you or something?"

"No, it's a gift. I, uh, I don't really know what they do."

"Really?" he asks, and his eyes light up. "Well then, let me explain. See, you put one of these in the middle of a room, and what it does is scan the surrounding area. I forget the actual figures, but it's strong enough to read most standard sized houses in their entirety. By the time it's done, it'll have downloaded the official plans for the property or area it's hit and be able to show you a map of every incoming and outgoing communication signal within the scan zone. Not only that, but you'll get to see exactly where the common incoming transmissions come from and where the outgoing ones go as well as the names of the service providers.

"You get all sorts of other data too—when the things were last used and so on. Most people buy them if they think someone's spying on them, but I've heard of all sorts of alternative uses. One woman I sold one to thought her partner was cheating on her. Came back to thank me for proving it and everything."

I can tell why his eyes lit up now. It was greed. That was his version of a sales pitch, designed to sell me on how great the thing is as a way to lighten the shock of how much he's going to try charging me. "Is that why it's called a ping box then? Because it checks host connections and stuff?"

"You'd think that, wouldn't you? No, it's because before the addition of the holographic screen, it used audio to tell you when it was done doing what you'd asked it to. The original prototype used a microwave bell as the alert sound. It was cheaper, because the creators had an old broken one lying around, and since it basically went *ping*, they went with it as codename for the project. That it fit well enough with the functionality was coincidental. Or so I'm told." He coughs, and adds, "So, it's a gift, huh? Is the recipient a bit paranoid?"

"Cassie? She can be. She's a PI, though, so..." I remember what Devin said, but it's too late. At the mere mention of her name, Joe has changed from aggressive salesman to angry balding man with all the cards.

"Cassie Tam," he spits. "I've met her. Well then, seeing as it's for my good friend Cassie, I'll do you a deal. Two hundred dollars."

"Two hundred," I repeat. "That seems a bit steep."

"This is top of the line tech," he replies. "Given her job, ol' Cassie would need something this good, and I just so happen to be the only licensed seller of this particular model in the city. Plus, that's with a discount."

"I think you could discount it a bit further."

"This isn't a marketplace, Missy. I don't do haggling."

"Would it help if I said Devin Carmichael sent me here to get it?"

He snorts out a laugh and replies, "Of course he did. Try again."

"He said if you try to charge me more than forty dollars, then I should tell you he still has the photo from Kansas."

Joe's face drops, and his confidence melts away. He lets out a *tch* and responds. "That man is going to bankrupt me. Fifty dollars."

"I thought you didn't haggle?"

"Forty is how much I pay for them. I need to make some sort of profit, don't I?"

I nod. "Okay, fifty seems fair."

"Like fuck it is," he grumbles and rings the purchase up on the till.

BY THE TIME I've made it to the office for day four of filming, I'm already nervous. Cassie sent me a long message detailing what the plan for today is, and I can't say I'm thrilled by it. I've taken myself off to the rest area under the guise of forgetting my breakfast and needing to make something quickly. In truth, I'm trying to get my bag in an optimal position to catch the whole room. Or as much of it as possible. Cassie is currently speaking to me over a wireless earpiece hooked up to my cell phone.

"Can you angle it to the left a little?"

I can't respond without arousing suspicion, so I just try. If there are any issues, I'll shake my head at the camera. In this case, I can bend the bag a little.

"Okay, that's coming through well here. I think... yeah, that should do it."

I nod.

"You better get back in there. Listen, I have the warrant sorted. It's one based around protection, which means I can use reasonable force. The moment he does what we expect him to, I'll be coming in with Bert. I'm a lot closer today too. Once we're there, we'll take care of him, okay? It's going to be tough today. Are you scared?"

I nod.

"If this works, it's going to get scarier. But don't worry. We're almost done."

I nod again, hang up the phone, and walk back to my desk with a cup of green tea in my hand. I blame Devin for that. Back at my desk, there's a new arrival on one of the risers. It's a little statue of a pineapple Damien dropped off with me on my way in. A few of the segments have cameras built in, the same as the bag. The idea is to show that Faye isn't being unreasonable when she carries out her part of the plan.

A quiet buzz from the corner of the room is followed by Faye glancing at her phone. Her breath catches, and she starts to shake a little. I really want to go over and comfort her right now, but we can't risk doing anything that will shift Mr. Graves's focus from her. So, I sit and watch, nervously biting my lower lip as she tries to calm herself. Eventually, she stands up and takes a few shaky steps toward her boss's office.

She knocks on the door. Rather than wait for an answer—which is his preferred reaction to his initial silence—she just pushes it opens. "You better have a good reason for entering uninvited," he says from within the room.

"I've had enough," Faye responds, barely audible even with the silence that's descended upon the room.

"You've *what*?" he responds, his voice gaining an edge of anger now.

"I said I've had enough," she repeats, louder this time. She balls her fists and continues, "The way you treat me is unacceptable. I'm reporting you to upper management."

"You will do no such thing," he roars, and the sound of his chair scraping rings out.

"I'm telling them *everything*," she says, her hand rising to her cheek. Then, time seems to speed up.

Faye slams Mr. Graves's office door and runs toward the rest room.

Mr. Graves exits his office, his face red with rage, and gives chase.

Faye shuts herself in the restroom, and Mr. Graves tries to barge in, but she holds the door shut just for a moment.

Some of the other ladies start screaming.

Mr. Graves forces the door open.

"You can't keep doing this to people," Faye yells.

The sound of a fist hitting flesh is enough to force me into action. I run in just in time to see Faye cowering on the floor, a trickle of blood running down her chin. I barely register the sound of a window breaking somewhere in the main room. Ignoring it, I yell, "Mr. Graves!"

When he turns, I throw the steaming-hot contents of my cup in his face and he stumbles back, clutching his eyes. "You bitch," he growls.

"Caw."

In a flash, Bert is leaping over me, using my shoulder to vault higher into the air. He hits Graves in the chest and pushes himself off, then comes in again and again, slamming himself against the man while Faye pushes herself further into the room.

The smell of a strong chemical breaks my concentration, and Cassie darts past me. Mr. Graves has his back to us now and doesn't see her come up behind him and force a rag over his face. He struggles, but between whatever she's soaked it in and Bert's continued pushing, he doesn't know where to focus. Within seconds, he's unconscious.

The moment he drops, Faye pushes to her feet and runs, tears streaming down her face. Without thinking, I follow, noting the screaming in the main part of the office has died down at last. When I catch up to her, she's already in the toilets slumped against the outside of a stall, sobbing uncontrollably.

I kneel and place my hand on her shoulder. "Hey. I'm Lori. Faye, listen. It's over now. It's all over."

She throws herself forward and wraps her arms around me in a hug as I whisper to her, "You did it. You are so, so brave."

IT TAKES THE police half an hour to get here. The result of which is when they do arrive, Faye and I are outside with the security guard I'd met on the first day. Meanwhile, Cassie and Bert remained upstairs watching Graves as he came to. I doubt he was happy with being faced with a combination of Bert and Cassie's Glock. He definitely wasn't happy to be dragged out in cuffs.

I felt like I was sleepwalking through the rest of my dealings with the police. I know they insisted Faye, Cassie, Damien, and I would all need to be spoken to separately, and so we were all made to travel in different vehicles. To their credit, shortly after Damien took one of the officers back to the NHNS office to review the paperwork and the most recent video, everything stopped feeling like an interrogation. The officers were fairly gentle in their queries. Mostly, they just let me confirm my side of things without much in the way of questioning.

Eventually, we're all let out to go our own way. Once we're outside, Cassie asks Faye, "Do you want me to give you a ride home?"

Faye nods. "Yes. Thank you. We should probably discuss how to pay your fee too."

Cassie shakes her head. "Don't you even think about it. Based on past behavior, I wouldn't expect Fast Ship to make it easy for you to get your wages this month. I'll be fine waiting. Just promise me if this ends up going to court, you'll tell them everything."

"I can do that," Faye says, and Cassie shows her to the passenger seat of her car.

She shuts the door and turns to me. "I'm worried about you."

Without thinking, I smile. "It's not often you're so direct."

She sighs and absently runs her fingers through her hair. "Yeah, well, I feel really guilty about this one. It was my idea to get you involved, and it really did put you at risk, eh?"

"It was, and it did. I'm glad I did it, though."

"Me too. Hey, do you want to go somewhere after I drop Faye home?"

I shake my head. "I'm sorry. I can't."

"Oh," she says and drops her head.

"Hey," I reply, using a finger to lift her gaze back to mine. "Don't worry. I'm not angry or anything like that. This whole thing has left me really drained. I need some time to process it all in my own way, that's all. It's a meet night tonight, so that'll help."

"I'd forgotten about that. Damn. I need to make a start on my taxes tonight."

I giggle. "That's fine. We're meeting up on Saturday, remember?"

"How could I forget?" She smiles. "Tomorrow then?"

"Tomorrow," I agree, and we share a quick kiss before parting. It sucks she'll probably worry now, but I really need to step back from the events of the last few days for a bit.

Chapter Four

THE FORSTER STREET Community Centre was always going to be the best place to hold the Tech Shift meets. It's spacious enough for us all to fit in on the evenings when we have a full roster, it's cheap, there's good parking, and it's not used as much as it should be, making it easy to book in. Since it came to me to arrange it all, that it's just down the road from my home is a bonus.

"You seem distracted. More than usual."

"I guess so," I reply, continuing to move the remaining chairs to the edges of the room.

Jane slides another pile of the same in next to mine and I sense her eyes on me. She's one of the few non-Tech Shifters we get at the meets, coming along to support her husband, Murphy. She's also one of my closer friends. "Argument with Cassie?"

I roll my eyes. "No, no. I was helping her with a case, actually. It got a bit rough, that's all."

"Ah. You want to talk about it?"

"Not really. I'm just gonna let Ink work it through, I think."

"Fair enough. Well, I'm here if you change your mind."

"Thank you."

The curtain on the stage at the back of the hall twitches and a metallic Alsatian comes trotting out. It hops off the stage and makes its way over to us. Jane leans down and gives her husband a stroke just as she'd do with a real dog. "Everyone will be getting here soon. I can finish up the last few chairs if you want to get changed."

I nod and grab my bag from next to the door and then walk up to the stage and slip behind the curtain. The change is all part of the ritual for me, helping me get into the right headspace. As such, I keep the Shifting routine pretty rigid. Everything goes on in a certain order, in a certain way. Okay, so the order is predetermined by the way the suits work, but the methods are mine and form an important part of the process.

I begin by gently removing the items from the oversized bag, and then start peeling my clothes off and packing them neatly in their place. I'm never naked underneath, not on meet nights; sometimes we have to share the changing space after all. As is always the case, I'm wearing a Lycra bodysuit. It's plain black to match Ink's general tone, and it comes with some light padding to help alter my body shape, making me seem more feline. The under layer is also important because, while a little more lightweight than it looks, Tech Shift gear *can* chafe the skin.

I run through a series of quick stretches to loosen myself up and make sure the suit is on properly, then grab the spine and head section from the floor. How people put this part on varies considerably. For me, I've found the most comfortable way is to gently press the back of the mask section into the plugs on my head, then press the neck section in, and finally the last two plugs at the base of my spine. From there, I move onto all fours, arch my back up, and tilt my head back as far as it will go. A sharp raising of my shoulders causes my head to connect with the hidden trigger that activates the magnetic pins. Doing it this way means the pins are all in place and ready to lock in without much wiggling or awkward reaching being required.

The spinal column detects when everything is connected, and the next part of the process begins automatically. The rolls of flexible metal running along the top of the column all splay out like octopus tentacles, then snap closed, wrapping tightly around my body. The motion conjures up a whole lot of different images for people. For me, being on the inside, it's like being encased in snap band bracelets. Once the tips of the individual segments have locked into the corresponding section on the spinal column, I pull the front of the mask down and push it into place.

With the main body done, I grab the front legs and stand them up, then move the back legs into place behind me. Using the chest plate on the front legs as a platform, and gripping the side of the legs for leverage, I lift one leg at a time and slide it into the back-leg section. Once I feel where my feet should rest, I reach back with my hands and manually lock them in place. Finally, I slide my hands into the front legs and let my body fall forward, locking the front shoulders into the spinal column. A quiet buzz runs through my ears as the legs connect to the power source, and I grip the pressure ball.

It's a small thing, but it's the sound accompanying the final step that's most important to me. It signifies the end of the change and lets me drift away into being Ink.

I STRETCH AND push through the curtain. Others have started to arrive, filling the room with an assortment of animals. They watch one another as they take in their surroundings.

I huff and leap from the stage, landing in a slow trot. Keeping low to the ground, I creep around the side of the room, my eyes on Daniel, a small tortoiseshell cat. He is still new to our community and unsure of himself. But he will learn.

Slowly, I creep around him and, just as he begins to turn, I thrust my shoulders into him and bound away. He looks funny when he scrambles to find me in the room. After three confused turns, his eyes to turn to me, and he starts to rush over.

I sit into my haunches, my tail flicking from side to side, and he slows. He approaches cautiously now, raising a paw toward me. I watch silently as he tentatively pushes it out but stops short of touching me when I yawn. When I don't move again, he tries rearing up, and I meet the movement, using one of my own paws to push him down. He rolls to the side and comes in again, this time trying to barge into me, but he over-pushes himself and slides over the top of my body.

Before I can react, he skitters away across the room and launches himself at another cat, who is watching us from the opposite corner of the room.

A gentle clicking of someone's tongue reaches my ears, and I turn to see Jane bent down, wriggling her fingers at me. She is the one human here tonight. She is not *my* human, but she is nice and has been with us longer than her. I walk to her and let her give me the fuss I deserve.

Content, I stalk back across the room and hop up onto the stage again, then lower myself onto my belly so I can let my paws hang over the edge. When the others come close, I may tap them. Just enough to let them know I'm here.

My tail flicks from side to side while I watch Jane and Murphy, the silly dog who likes to chase his ball. I am happy, but I miss Cassie when she is not here.

She is mine.

Perhaps she will come next time.

STEPPING BACK INTO being Lori is jarring sometimes. But by the time I've followed the Tech Shifting process in reverse, I'm there. As is often the case, everything seems a lot clearer now.

We did good today. We helped someone and made sure the good guys are on their way to winning. Maybe I was a little annoyed Cassie put me in that position, but she had good intentions. And I could have said no. The main thing is, I feel like I might actually sleep well tonight.

"Feeling any better?" Jane asks as I emerge from behind the curtain, now dressed normally again.

I nod. "Taking a break from everything helps. A lot. It always amazes me how much my mind manages to work out in the background while I'm Ink. It's like..."

"Like you aren't even aware you're working through it all, because you're so deep in the headspace?" I nod, and Jane smiles. "It's the same for Murph. You get to step away, and it just works itself out for you."

"Exactly."

"HE REALLY DENIED it all?" I ask, stirring my latte.

Cassie smiles. "At first. Then they showed him some highlights from the videos. He wasn't happy about that.

Even less so when they explained the footage was legally usable. His lawyer made a call to Graves Sr., and in the end, he agreed to plead guilty to all charges. He'll likely get a reduced sentence for doing so, but the PD are pushing for jail time anyway. If anyone else comes forward now, he could end up in a far worse position."

"Good."

"As soon as he hit her, I started running, so I didn't see what you did until last night. You know, that was pretty dangerous, throwing your drink at him."

"Yeah, I guess it was."

"What happened to not being able to put yourself in a position where you may get the abuse?"

"When it came down to it, I knew it was the right thing to do. I don't know, maybe knowing we had the footage and you were on your way helped make me braver?"

"You were already brave, Lori. The way you stuck with it, especially with how it was affecting you? *That* was more than most would manage."

"Maybe. I do admire you, though."

Cassie tilts her head curiously. "Really? Why?"

"Because you see stuff like this all the time. Whether it's related to people, businesses, or even privacy, you're around abuse all the time. You know it doesn't always end happily, you don't even try to lie to yourself about that, yet you keep going back in there."

She shrugs and takes a mouthful of coffee. "It's my job. Besides, someone has to do it."

"It's more than that. You're hard to it. You stand strong and don't hesitate. You keep fighting. I admire that because you put yourself out there for people, not just because it's your job, but because you want to see the right side win as much as possible. You're like a real-life hero."

Cassie takes my hand and gives it a squeeze. "Thank you. It makes me happy when someone appreciates what I do. But I'm no hero. Believe me, I've made plenty of mistakes over the last few years. And I've had to do some really nasty things and work with some even worse people. I think that disqualifies me from the hero category."

"So, you mess up and do bad things sometimes. That just makes you human. We don't live in a comic book. In this world, the best heroes are human, mistakes and all. You're a hero to me, and you're not going to change that with some stubborn self-depreciation."

"*Ǎi*. You are impossible, you know that?"

"Well, that makes two of us. Oh, yeah, hang on." I reach into my bag and produce a shiny red gift bag. "Sorry it isn't wrapped; I didn't have the chance. The bag is nice, though."

Cassie reaches across and takes it, then gives me a suspicious look. "Remember, I said not to make a big fuss."

"I know. Don't worry, it wasn't hugely expensive or anything. Come on, open it. You'll like it."

Cassie raises an eyebrow at me and opens the bag and peers in. She pauses, reaches inside, and pulls out the box. "These things cost a couple of hundred dollars."

"Normally, yes. This one didn't."

"Lori, I really love that you've put some thought into this, but this is way over the price limit."

"No, no, look, I knew you'd do this. I've got the receipt and everything. It's in the bottom there. In case it doesn't work."

Cassie rummages through the bag and pulls out a small slip of paper. She reads it silently to herself and then asks, "How the hell did you get Joe Farrah to sell you a ping box for fifty dollars? You didn't mention me, I assume?"

"I kinda did, yeah. He's not your biggest fan, is he?"

She smiles and shakes her head. "No. No, he is not."

"Okay. So, you remember how low I was after day three? Well, I didn't go straight home. I kinda needed something to distract myself and put some distance between me and what was happening. And...well...I had no clue what to get you, so I figured taking a walk and trying to figure it out would help."

"What made you think of a ping box?"

"Honestly? I didn't. I was staring dejectedly at windows and I spotted someone walking by who I thought might be able to help."

"Charlie?" she tries.

"Oh, no. I *do* want to meet her, and you were right when you showed me the photograph. I *had* seen her around once or twice, but...I mean, do you really think I'd ask your ex-girlfriend for gift advice for you?"

"I don't know, maybe?" I give Cassie a look that basically tells her she's nuts, and she asks, "Okay then, who did you see?"

"Devin Carmichael."

Cassie stops mid-swallow and places her mug back on the table. "Devin Carmichael."

"Yeah. So, I ran after him, and we had a bit of a chat. He said some really interesting stuff, actually." I notice the corners of Cassie's mouth twitch nervously and can't help but smile as I continue. "I told him what I needed help with, and he said you'd probably really like one of these. He sent me to Joe Farrah and told me what to say to get the price down."

"And what's that?"

"Something about him having a photo of Joe from Kansas. Any idea what that's about?"

"No clue."

"Yeah, so he cut it right down."

"Huh. So, when you say Devin said some interesting things..."

I laugh. "Someone has a guilty conscience, don't they? He happened to mention something about you talking to him about talking to me. Care to explain?"

"I...thought that, maybe, if he spoke to you about what happened with your brother, it would help you get closure. Or, I don't know, at least see it wasn't personal on Devin's part. He wouldn't do it, though, and in the end, I figured out it would have probably done more harm than good."

"You had no intention of telling me either, did you?"

"No. Sorry."

I breathe out a short, relaxed laugh and reply, "Well, I can't say it was one of your best ideas. But you meant well. It was sweet. In a totally misguided kinda way."

"You're not mad?"

"No. But it *was* a little naughty. So, I was thinking, if you're really sorry about it, you might want to make it up to me. Maybe with a little game?"

"What sort of game?"

"I promised to keep to two limits today. No more than two presents and no more than one hundred dollars in total, right? Well, I've spent half of that so far, and you only have one present. So, I thought we could do a bit of shopping. If you win the game, then you get to choose the second present. If *I* win, then you have to accept whatever I choose."

Cassie taps the table with her fingers, her eyes betraying a slight nervousness. "What sort of present did you have in mind if you won?"

"That's a surprise for *if* I win. But I promise you'll like it. And if *you* win, then you have total control over it and can make sure it's something you like, right?"

"I *did* say you could spend one hundred on two presents." She thinks it over and continues, "Okay. Okay, so what's the game?"

"I'm going to ask you one question. I'll give you one clue. And you'll get one guess. It'll be about me, and it'll test whether you've been paying attention. It *is* something you'd know."

Cassie smiles, confidence filling her face as she nods her consent. "I can do that. You know how I pay attention to every little detail, eh."

"I like how confident you are. Okay then, here's the question. What is my middle name?"

Cassie's face drops a little. "What's my clue?"

"It begins with 'N'."

"N."

Cassie sits back and starts drumming her fingers on the table again. Her face tenses up a little as she concentrates, probably running multiple conversations through her head. Quickly, a smile creeps across her face, and she says, "Got it."

I open my hands to her to signal she can answer, and she says, with complete certainty, "Nancy."

"Same as my nan?" She nods, and I smile. "Nope."

Her face drops again. "It's not? Then what is it?"

"None. I don't have a middle name."

"That's cheating," she huffs and crosses her arms in a state of childish defiance.

"Of course it's not. Remember when you gave me the Case Tool to complete, back when I hired you? It asks for my middle name in the basic fields. What do you think I put in there?"

Cassie drops her head into her hands and giggles. "None. You put None, didn't you?"

"Yup. Which means *I* get to choose your second gift."

"Okay, fine. So, where are we heading for this?"

I point over her shoulder at the line of stores across the street from our table outside Cartwright's. "Third from the left. My left."

I hear Cassie swallow hard and can't suppress the giggle as she turns back, her face awash with absolute horror as she points out the obvious. "That's a lingerie store."

"It is. I was thinking last night, and I realized something. I've never seen you in anything other than some very basic sleepwear. I was thinking maybe something lacy, but I'll be nice and let you have a say in what we buy."

"I thought you said I'd like this," she says, pointing an accusatory finger at me. "You promised."

I wink and let a mischievous glint rise to my eyes. "I promise you'll enjoy how much *I* like the gift."

And with that, Cassie's cheeks start to redden, and she buries her face in her coffee mug. Even if she finds a way to talk me out of it now, her reaction is enough to keep me smiling.

SHADOWS OF THE

PAST

Chapter One

CASSIE

I force my hand up under the headset and scratch behind my ear. This is part of why I could never become a Virtual Reality Junkie; it's really not all that immersive for me. Looking around me, the small room is everything it should be in reality. The layout is simple, uncluttered, and the focus is drawn solely to the altar at the far end. That, more so than the rest of the simulation, is ornate. The three-drawer unit is simple enough, but it's built to look like a nineteenth-century cabinet, much like you'd still find in a lot of Chinese homes. The cabinet on top is colored in the same dark-brown hue, but features a painted floral pattern wrapping around the two doors.

I reach out and let my hand linger on the design—because I'm not entirely immune to the wonder associated with these realistic simulations—and the sensors in the gloves I'm wearing send a little signal into my fingertips, triggering the sensation of touching the wood in my brain. I sigh. "It's not as magical when you *can't* forget it's not real."

The doors open with ease, revealing a photograph of my father. It's one from the year of his death. He's in his police uniform, standing proudly with his wide, Chow Yun-Fat smile. Even when things were at their worst, he could always find a reason to smile, and the simple act made things seem so much better. I guess it's why Mom chose this photo. Either that or she thought it hurt me seeing him in uniform. I wouldn't put it past her.

"We never were a religious family," I say, pulling the first drawer open and unpacking the contents. "So many who came before us converted to Christianity, but it didn't feel like the right fit to you, I remember you saying that. You never discouraged anyone from exploring religion, but in the end, your attitude to it all made it easier for me to not give the subject much thought. Grandpa, on the other hand, was a traditionalist. The stories he used to tell were...well, he told you them too. Honestly, though, it wasn't until the reading of your will that I realized how many relatives we still had in China and Hong Kong, much less how many still followed the traditional beliefs. That's the real advantage of the forced virtual burial system. Anyone can come from anywhere at any time, as long as they can prove they have a reason. It's funny, but even knowing you didn't believe in this stuff yourself, even knowing it's mostly for the family I barely knew, it'd seem wrong not to do the full thing."

I smile and shake my head. "I say the same thing every year, don't I? I don't know, maybe it just makes it easier to get through those initial memories, eh? I promised you last year I wouldn't keep apologizing, so I won't this time."

Stepping back, I take a moment to examine my handiwork. The photo cabinet is now presiding over a number of items. Or virtual representations of them at least.

Sat in front of it, there's a paper-wrapped burger from the local food truck we used to go to back in Vancouver, as well as a bottle of the shitty beer he used to love after a hard day at work. To the left is an unlit incense stick, and to the right is a small bowl containing a couple of sheets of Xiaoyin, the traditional ghost money burned for close ancestors. In front of all of that is an unbranded box of matches, chosen because Dad not only preferred them to lighters, but refused to buy expensive brands of things so simple. The offerings should really be given in bi-monthly visits, or on the Quingming and Ghost Festivals, but I only get to visit the place once a year for the anniversary, so I do them all in one go. It's a special occasion for me, so that much fits with tradition at least.

The smell of incense is filling my nose already. When I rent the VR set each year, I ask for the sensors in the headgear to be switched off. I'll allow the hand zappers, but only because when I tried to do the altar setup without them, it was surprisingly disorienting. There is no way I'm letting some computer hat blast my head, though, so I lit some real stuff before I logged in. *It must be about halfway through now if I'm getting the scent this strongly.*

I slide open the matchbox, light the virtual stick, and toss the match into the bowl. Everything lights perfectly the first time. Part of me would be more willing to accept the illusion if things sometimes went wrong, but then I'd only moan about what the point of a simulated burial system is if it can't improve on reality. *The modern world just can't win with me.*

I bow my head and close my eyes. "A lot has changed since last year. I met somebody. Her name's Lori. She was a client, actually. I helped her figure out what happened to her brother. You would have liked her, I think. She really cares about me, more than I'm used to these days. I care about her more than I'm..." I shake my head. "I didn't realize how much I needed someone like her. Especially now. I knew some things here were similar to Vancouver, but I didn't expect New Hopeland to be *different* in the ways it is. There were so many things I had no clue about until recently. I don't really know how I feel about it. And part of me wants to walk away from it all, find somewhere where the corruption is simple, but I can't. I never could, eh? Not while there are people to protect. Not while Lori is here."

A low buzz rings in my ears for a second and then fades into footsteps that come to an abrupt halt. A voice I haven't heard for six years asks, "You're still here?"

I open my eyes, but don't turn around. Given the number of duplicate memorial rooms you get with an Al Berry Funeral plan, she could have just picked an empty one. She's come here on purpose. "A case overran."

Mom sniffs in disgust. "It would be a case, wouldn't it?"

"There is somebody at your door," a synthesized voice says in my ear, but I mute it.

"Stop that," I snap. "Not in front of Dad's grave."

"Virtual shrine."

I turn and shoot her my second favorite glare. Yes, second favorite because she's not worth my number one. "You know what I mean. Plus, you won't let me have any of the ashes, so it's not like I have a choice but to come here. You do."

She smirks. "Yes, I do. And I choose to come here as per my husband's wishes. And as to the ashes, why would I send a part of him to his murderer?"

Now that one hurt. "I didn't—" I manage, but she cuts me off.

"You didn't pull the trigger. But you may as well have. You just never knew when to quit."

I want to fight back. To say something. Anything. But something stops me. Mom was always good at masking the tone of her voice, but her mask wasn't foolproof. The headsets won't map tears, but they do map eye movements. Even now, I recognize the way the edges of Mom's eyes are tightening. So, I simply walk past her toward the exit point. I have someone at my door, after all. Before I can leave, something stops me. I have to try. "I've met someone."

"Do you expect me to be happy for you?" she asks, her voice near monotoned, but carrying the weight of a lot of hurt.

I turn my head downward, now unable to even admire the detail work on the wooden floor and walk through the exit door.

MY VIEW GOES black, signaling the disconnect from the server, and I slip the headset off. Sure enough, there's somebody knocking on my door.

"All right, I'm coming," I yell, wiping my eyes on my sleeve. I push up to my feet and toss the headset onto the couch. The rental set is sturdy, and the couch is soft, so it's fine. I stop short of letting my apparent guest in when I notice Bert sitting on the kitchen worktop, staring at the door. "Something wrong?"

"Caw."

Bert's tone is neutral, and his mechanical body has dropped into a relaxed pose. I frown but turn and open the door anyway. The reason for Bert's unusual behavior becomes clear immediately. Standing in the hallway is Dr. Faraday, one of the technicians at Familiar Enterprises. She is also, much like Bert, an AI. Unlike my shiny little gargoyle, though, she looks entirely human, and consequently, very few people are aware of what she is. "Miss Tam. May I come in?" she asks.

"Sure," I reply and walk back into the apartment. "I'm guessing from the lack of a phone call this isn't about Bert?"

Dr. Faraday shuts the door and leans against it, her body giving off a surprising amount of apprehension. "I wish it were."

"Huh. In that case, this is where I'd normally offer a drink. Do you drink anything?"

"I can, but only because it relaxes people more if I'm seen to be doing human things. I don't technically need to. Would you prefer if I did?"

"Not now I know you don't need to, no. The office is that table in the middle of the room. Grab a seat."

"Thank you, Miss Tam."

I watch Dr. Faraday take the nearest seat and immediately move to the one opposite. Despite knowing it's probably a little rude, I can't help but drop my elbows onto the table and lower my chin onto my crossed hands. "You weren't this formal last time I met you. It feels unnatural."

"It was a different situation. In many respects, I held the position of power. Now, I am in need of help."

"Not everything is a power struggle. Quit it, anyway. It's freaking me out. If you feel like you have to use my name, Cassie or Caz is fine. And no, I don't have a preference."

She nods and tightens her scruffy ponytail. "Very well. Caz it is then."

"So. You said you need my help. What kind of help?"

"Protection, partially. And for you to find someone."

I raise an eyebrow and tap the fingers of my top hand on the lower one. "Sounds complicated. Are both things connected, or are they two separate issues?"

"Yes, they're both connected. I'm being...stalked. I need you to find out who by."

I drop my hands to the table and sigh. Complicated was right. "Do you mind if I grab a coffee myself?" Faraday nods and I make my way to the kitchen. Even with the table so close to the kitchen, my kettle is currently running at the volume known as "stubbornly boisterous," so when I continue, I have to raise my voice to make sure I'm heard. "First things first, why do you think you're being stalked?"

"I wasn't sure at first. I'd catch things out of the corner of my eyes, familiar shapes and so on, but I brushed it off as part of the daily routine. I leave home, go to work, and come home again."

Huh. I'd presumed she just stayed at the office. That's interesting. Let's just treat this like she's human. "Let me guess. You take the same routes to work and back each day, so you figured you were catching people with similar habits."

"Yes. I keep fairly regular hours, the same as most people. And you've seen the offices. Quite aside from the sheer number of staff, there are plenty of other businesses nearby. So, I made a game of it. I started trying to take note of the people around me, to see if I could figure out who I was spotting. But that one person was always just out of sight. It was as if they were intentionally avoiding me getting a good look at them."

"And you're certain there's only one person doing this, and it's not multiple similar sized people you're noticing?"

"Yes."

"I suppose, all things considered, you'd be able to tell, right? Your eyes would be like Bert's."

"Actually, no. Bert's purpose is his own, and he is built to be suitable for his particular role. I, on the other hand, am built to imitate humans, and that comes with certain limitations. While my eyes operate in a similar way to Bert's, their power is more akin to the average person."

I finish pouring my coffee and make my way back to the table. "That opens up the possibility of this being just a case of someone taking the same route as you each day."

Faraday shakes her head. "No, they're definitely following me. I know, because I tricked them."

"Okay, explain."

"Well, I was heading home, and started catching sight of the *shape* again. Rather than continue on my normal route, I took a shortcut down an alley. Yes, it was risky, but I'm familiar enough with the area to know I wasn't getting closed in. I only take the longer route normally because I prefer the scenery. Anyway, I kept going, and by this point, being out of the crowds, I could hear their footsteps. When they stopped partway down I...I couldn't stop myself. I turned and saw them. Sort of."

"Sort of?"

"They were wearing a dark hoodie and had turned away to look at something. A security camera, I think. Regardless, the hood was up, and they weren't looking at me, so I couldn't see their face."

"And what did you do then?"

"I ran. I knew for certain someone had been following me then, and human limitations being what they are—" she flexes her fingers a little and sighs "—I'm not exceptionally strong. My hands are better suited to my allocated job than to fighting."

"Okay," I reply, keeping my voice as light as possible. "When you saw this person, did you notice anything at all that may help identify them? Any clear indicators of gender, any standout physical traits?"

"No, I'm sorry. The hoodie was baggy enough to hide their shape well."

"That makes it a little difficult, but if they were looking at a camera, then maybe we'll get lucky. I'll be honest with you; I'm going to have a lot of questions. *But*...your safety is the most important thing right now. I assume you've finished work for the day?" She nods. "How does it feel when you're there? Do you think you'll be safe in the office?"

"Definitely. I've not noticed anything once I'm in there, only on the walks to and from."

"And at home?"

"I'm not sure. They are clearly aware of where I live, though I'm not sure if they know which apartment."

"That would have been my next question; are you in a house or an apartment? As a setup, New Hopeland's security laws for apartment blocks do give you some built-in protection. But I don't want to rule out the possibility they know. Which is where things get complicated for me. If I'm going to be offering protection, I need to get some paperwork filed with the PD to grant me certain *rights*. The person I'd need to sign off on them is the captain, Andrew Hoover, and I know for certain he's not going to be available now until the morning."

"So, you can't offer anything immediate in terms of protection?"

"There's a clause in the middle of the legal jargon meaning I can step in if needed, but I need some things from you first. I assume you have a Wi-Fi connection at your place?"

"Of course."

I down my coffee and stand. "How did you get here this evening?"

"I walked."

"Did you notice this person following you on the way over?"

"No."

"Still, better to be on the safe side." I head to the kitchen and grab one of my Case Tools. I hand it to Faraday and explain, "This contains a copy of my standard paperwork. It has a holographic keyboard built in. Once you're home, I'll need you to fill out everything with as much detail as possible. When you hit send, it'll transfer everything to me securely. I can pick it up again tomorrow. Do you have a cell?"

"Yes, here."

I pull my own cell out and open an app, then tap the phone against Faraday's. Within seconds, it gives a notification the transfer is complete. "You'll have seen this before. It's the loaned summoning app."

"Ah, yes. How long is the loan set to?"

"One week. It works well, so if you feel like there's something wrong, hit the app and Bert will come to step in with me following closely behind. Make sure you complete the Case Tool first if you can. I can argue my way to us needing to act if we need to, but it's going to be less messy if I have it on file you're hiring me, and most importantly why, before we do anything."

"I understand. I'll complete it as soon as I'm home."

"I'll drive you. If nothing else, I want to see how to get to your apartment just in case. Oh, and I'll need a key for tomorrow. Don't worry if you don't have a spare, I'll be picking you up in the morning and dropping you at the office. We can sort the times out on the way."

"Thank you, Caz. You can ask whatever you need while you drive too."

I shake my head. "I'll leave that for tomorrow. Once I have the Case Tool to review, I'll have a better idea what I *need* to ask. Besides, if I'm playing bodyguard, you're going to be seeing a lot of me. It's best to leave ourselves something to talk about, eh?"

CAPTAIN HOOVER CHECKS over the details I've entered on the tablet, and grunts. "It all seems in order. Still...a stalker. You'd expect Dr. Faraday to come to us first."

I shrug. "I thought so too. I'll be asking her why she didn't, don't worry about that." *Though I suspect it's because I know what she is.*

"If it's down to something fixable, let me know, yeah? I get there's client confidentiality involved, but I'd like to think the PD is viewed as reliable by most people."

"Depending on her answer, sure."

"Okay, so you know the drill by now. The usual caveats apply, but this allows you to use suitable force in cases of reasonable doubt in relation to the safety of your client. Unless things really go bad, though, shoot to kill is *not* your first course of action."

I smile. "It never is, Hoove."

"I know, but I have to give you at least part of the spiel, or I get hauled over the coals. You see the guy dressed to the nines talking to Devereaux?"

I glance over Hoove's shoulder to see there is indeed a well-dressed man talking to the young corporal. "Yeah, what about him?"

"He's from the committee responsible for law enforcement in Utah. He's here to make sure we're dotting as many i's and crossing as many t's as possible *without impeding on the smooth and lawful running of the business.*"

I get the impression the last part was the good captain mocking the way the guy speaks and smile. "Sounds like a fine, upstanding member of the team."

Hoove laughs. "Sounds like a prick, you mean."

"That's the one. I always get those two mixed up."

"Sure, you do. Who are you gonna get to sign onto the temporary will? The license doesn't fully come into force until you get that sorted."

"One of these days, I'll get a full will put together, then I won't have to bother," I grumble. "I'm gonna ask Lori. Not sure how she'll take it. It makes the risk that much more real, eh?"

"It's always tough on partners. Well, good luck with that. You're about as done as you can be until you speak with her."

"Not like I intend on enacting the thing," I say, casually waving the thought off as I get to my feet. "Thanks, Hoove. I'll leave you to get back to your pet suit."

I leave the police station, intentionally avoiding the people I know. I'm not feeling anti-social, honest, I just want to get stuck into this. In my experience, stalker cases have the tendency to blow up pretty quickly, and I don't want to leave too many opportunities for that to happen.

When I make it back to my car, I pause to send Lori a message asking to meet up for lunch, then start the engine and make the drive to Dr. Faraday's apartment block. She left me with her key after I dropped her at work and gave me a quick introduction with the door security when I picked her up, so it's easy enough to get up to her place on the fifth floor. I'd be lying if I said I wasn't curious as to how a robot who's pretending to be a human lives. I didn't go into the apartment last night, only as far as the door, so this should be an experience.

The key itself is interesting because it's a fairly recent model. Yeah, I know, the world must be pretty exciting if I'm learning about models of keys. In my line of work, it's important to know, so I don't really have much choice in the matter. In this case, it looks like the ornate ones you used to get with five lever mortice locks, but it's bigger, thicker, and houses a run of circuitry on its underside. I slot it flat onto the pad-like lock, and after a few seconds of scanning, the door clicks open.

When I step in, I'm a little surprised, though I don't really know why. I had no real preconceived notions about what I'd find. Dr. Faraday holds a high-end position in Familiar Enterprises, so why wouldn't this be what her place would look like?

"Don't lie to yourself, you were expecting minimalist living with oversized charger cables," I tell myself, and reach into my pocket. I pull a little metal box out of my pocket and place it on the glass coffee table sitting neatly in front of the luxurious faux-leather couch near the totally-not-jealousy-inducing massive television. It seems like a good spot because, while not the center of the room, it should be roughly the center of the actual apartment.

I tap the button on the top of the box, and a small holographic display lights up. "Ping box. Initiate area scan, search for all outgoing signals and recipient registrations. Include both active and currently inactive signals. Notify once complete."

The box lets out a gentle beep and a single line starts moving back and forth across the display like a windscreen wiper. Confident it'll pick up on whatever I need it to, I treat myself to a tour of Dr. Faraday's home.

The main room features the TV area, which I now note seems to come complete with a high-end entertainment system. The drawers, which I'm guessing contain discs and USB sticks, are locked with a number pad. At the opposite side of the room sits a full-size computer, a laptop, and a tablet, because you can never have too much access to the net, right? There's also a small balcony outside, so I head out to check for likely places Dr. Faraday could be seen from.

As it happens, that's not the most likely scenario. The familiar signs of the standard metal guards are all around the balcony's framework, and her Case Tool entries *did* say she uses them every night. The nearby buildings are constructed without windows facing the block, and the space below isn't going to offer too much of a view unless someone backs way up, and Dr. Faraday is on the balcony itself. Even then, she's gonna have a better view of the street below than anyone on it has of her.

Satisfied, I re-enter the main room and notice for the first time there's art on the inside of the door. It looks like an impressionist piece of some sort; it's not a Monet or a Cezanne, and it's definitely not an original, but the style fits. "No, it can't be from the era. It's a sunset over a modern city. I can see the skyscrapers."

But that's not important, so I head to the kitchen. Much like the living area, it's modern, the items are made by decent brands, and there isn't really much there of note. Though it does seem strange the fridge and freezer are well stocked with food and drink. "I wonder how much of it goes to waste?"

Next stop, the bedroom, with its fitted wardrobes, double bed, and silken sheets. A quick browse of the wardrobes shows mostly business suits, a couple of lab coats, some jeans, fitted tops, dresses. Nothing out of the ordinary, and nothing seems out of place. I decide against checking her drawers because, as it stands, I'm guessing they'll contain perfectly normal underwear. Under the bed I find a few boxes of papers, all covered in handwritten notes. The handful I check contain a mix of complex schematics and lists of reference numbers.

My final stop is the bathroom, which is situated behind the wall nearest the couch. Bath, shower, toilet, sink, heated flooring, and some basic supplies in a small cabinet. I tap my fingers on the sink and look at my reflection in the mirror. "It's all very fitting. Nothing is too low-end to seem out of place with her position, but nothing is ridiculously high-end either. Think. If you didn't know *what* she was, how would *you* take all this."

I walk out of the bathroom and relax onto the couch to wait for the ping box to finish. "Everything would be what I expected. Maybe if I didn't know where she worked, or what her job was, the computers would seem too much, but it's not unheard of for people to splash out. The art doesn't really fit, but people with money tend to have at least one interest falling outside their usual expertise. Could that be it, though? Could someone have seen this place and thought she was trying too hard to seem like a typical New Hopeland technician? Maybe it tipped them off that there's more to her?"

The ping box lets out a melodious tone to let me know it's done with its sweep, and the screen flashes up a "view results" button. I tap it and am treated to a copy of the basic apartment layout, taken from the official planning documents. There are small indicators in each room, telling me where there are things capable of sending signals. I start with the balcony as it only has one target, and the screen confirms that, as I expected, it's simply a system to let the building staff know if the shutters are down, up, or jammed. The bedroom apparently has a camera built into the lights, but the indication is it hasn't been used for ten years, so I'm assuming the room is registered as a bedroom and so falls under the privacy guidelines for security monitoring.

The same can be said for the bathroom. There's no camera, as there's no way the room could ever have been anything else, but there are a number of small transmitters confirming when water is turned on and off. The data stream is constant, so that'll be to alert the building staff if someone is either overdoing it, or if there's a leak. The kitchen has a security camera built into the lighting, which is listed as active but not currently in use, meaning it'll only turn on if needed. Records show it hasn't been on for months.

The living room looks like a hotbed of activity. The computing stuff all gets regular use-and-transmit data through the building's Wi-Fi and Ethernet services, which is as expected. The TV is also hooked up to the Internet. All four contain cameras that have been used to transmit data recently, though the indication is they were activated manually. Two security cameras are built into the lights. I look up and smile. "Of course I didn't see them. It's all recessed LED lighting with auto adjustment angling. They'll look just like the lights unless I turn them on. Fancy."

Again, the cameras are active but not currently in use, with the last known use being in the far past. Which means no one is spying on Dr. Faraday through her internal systems. "Wait...what's that by the door?"

I look at the indicator on the screen and give it a tap, only to be told there's another camera and an Internet enabled monitor running constantly somewhere in the room. I turn and stare at the door, but all I can see is the painting. "Ah, wait a minute."

I walk back to the door and examine the painting closely. It's sticking out from the door in a box-like fitting. And there's a small button on the bottom. I give it a tap and the painting flickers off to be replaced with a view of the hallway outside. Satisfied, I turn the security system off and head back to the ping box so I can check the list of recipients associated with the transmissions going out from the apartment, in case something isn't what it seems. No such luck. They're all registered to the building, Familiar Enterprises, a popular Internet service provider, and the local government security system.

"Ping box, save data and shut down."

Beep. Beep. Beep. The holographic screen disappears.

"Okay, so it means either nobody is monitoring the Doc using modern tech inside the apartment, or this is an inside job from the building or FE Limited. Right. Let's see if Lori's replied."

I exit Dr. Faraday's home and head back to my car. I had to leave my cell phone in there so the ping box didn't pick up on it, but that wasn't a bad thing. It was useful not to have any distractions while I looked around. It seems like Lori wants to meet up at Cartwright's. Sounds good to me.

"YOU HAVEN'T GOT a will?" Lori asks, her eyes scanning the file that's open on my tablet. It's her first question since she started reading it, which is probably not a good sign.

I shrug and sip a little bit of caffeinated heaven from my mug. "I guess it just never seemed like a priority. When I was just starting out, I didn't even think about it. I was young, eh?"

"You're still young."

"Younger then. The point is, I had no reason to make one. I was living with my parents, so I figured they'd sort it out *if* something happened to me. And when I came here...well, who was I going to leave my stuff to? Or for that matter, what did I really have left to leave? A couple of sets of clothes, and an old tablet and phone? I had to fund moving down here myself, as well as buying upgrades for my tools. It meant getting rid of a lot of the older stuff I'd have taken with me otherwise."

"Huh. I guess I never really considered the idea that you'd have had trouble with money early on. I mean, you've had a couple of well-paying cases over the last few months, right? You must've had the same back in Vancouver."

"Not quite. I was good, but the cases were *mostly* a lot lower end than I get here. It's part of the charm of New Hopeland; there's always a shit hole to dig for gold in. But even then, it's a little difficult. I still have some debts, for one. They're controlled debts, loans and stuff like that, but they're there. And yeah, I do have a nice little amount in the bank right now, but I can't use it freely because I never know when I'm gonna hit a dry spell or a low-paying run."

Lori nods. "Plus, there's your mortgage pay-off plan. You know if you ever get in trouble you can come to me, right?"

I sigh and absently scratch my fingers through my hair. "I figured you'd say something like that. It's why I've not really mentioned money too much before. It's not that I don't appreciate it, but…"

"But it would be a cold day in hell before you swallow your pride and ask for help." Lori laughs and shakes her head. "You're a stubborn one."

"There's nothing wrong with being stubborn. Besides, I'm comfortable in my routine. I know how to handle the money, I have savings to use when it's tough, and I keep on top of what I need to."

"You make it sound like there wouldn't be much to leave in a will."

"There isn't. Most of my stuff is probably useless to anyone outside the business, and even then, it's hardly top of the line. The car is nice, though."

Lori rolls her eyes. "Yes, your car is lovely."

I smile. "You act like I mention it a lot."

"Oh, you may have praised it once or twice."

"Hey, I can't help that I'm proud of the thing. Or proud I'm able to keep the thing running. Anyway, Bert's my main concern. Without a will, everything would go to the State. Can you imagine what would happen if the government tried to seize him?"

Lori waggles a finger at me and takes a bite from her blueberry muffin. She doesn't even finish swallowing before she speaks, leaving her voice amusingly muffled. "I know what you're doing, you know. You saw my reaction to this, and you're trying to deflect the conversation with humor. Cassie, you're trying to get me to sign off on a last will and testament for you."

"*Temporary* will," I reiterate.

Lori wipes her mouth with her hand and continues, "Temporary or not, the fact you're bringing this to me means you're working on a case where it's going to be potentially needed."

"No, it means it's a case where the local laws require me to have one."

"Still."

I lower my chin to my hand, tilt my head, and smile. "You're worried about me."

"Of course I'm worried about you. You want me to agree to being part of a legally required *will*."

"You didn't seem this worried about me during the Kitsune case."

"Okay. One, I had *no* idea how risky that case was going to get. And two, maybe I care about you a little more than I realized." Lori holds her hands out and regains the volume she lost when she mumbled her second reason. "Anyway, the main point is, if the law requires it, then it *might* be needed, right? Like, it might be closer to being a 'definitely' than normal?"

Don't question the "and two." You aren't ready yet. I sigh and push my hair back behind my ears. "Okay, I'll be honest here. Yes, this sort of case *can* have certain risks. In a way, I'll be playing bodyguard as well as detective. But it doesn't mean other cases aren't risky too. Wait. That doesn't help, does it?"

"No, no. Do continue."

I take a frustrated gulp of milky courage and try again. "Yes, there are risks. But it's rare for anything to actually happen." I catch Lori's raised eyebrow and clarify. "Anything outside the norm. And by that, I mean normal for most PIs, not normal for me the last few months. You can verify it if you like. Look up local cases like this online. Not many go bad. Look, I *honestly* don't expect the will to be needed in the way you're worrying about. It's just something the law requires me to have."

"Is everything okay? Can we get you anything else?" the waitress cuts in.

"I could go for the same again," I tell her and glance at Lori. "You?"

"Sure," Lori replies, and the waitress makes her way back to the counter. Once she's returned with the drinks—which were mysteriously already ready for us—and headed off to the next table, Lori tells me, "I'm going to say something, and I want you to promise not to freak out, okay?"

"Okay," I reply, keeping my voice slow.

"Why not use this as a way to reconnect with your mom?"

I blink. "You do remember what I told you about visiting my father's grave?"

"I do."

"Then what would make you think I'd want to do that?"

"You miss her."

"I do not," I state, my voice a little too high and shrill for my liking. Once I shrug off the embarrassment of having drawn the attention of our fellow patrons, I repeat, but quieter, "I do not."

"Cassie, you let your guard down around me a lot more now. I saw it in your eyes when you were telling me about it."

"I *don't* miss her."

"There's that famous Tam stubbornness again."

"And even if I did," I add, ignoring her comment, "she clearly doesn't miss me."

"Cassie, how late were you?"

"Not that late," I concede. "Maybe thirty minutes?"

"Have you ever been late before?"

"Once or twice."

"And she never turned up like that?" I shake my head and Lori asks, "Was your dad stubborn? Like you are, I mean, not in a work sense. Be honest with me."

Seeing where this might be going, I open my mouth to shoot down the idea, but the words die in my mouth. Finally, I reply with a simple, "No."

"Then where do you think you get it from? From what little you've told me about her, I think you and your mom may be...well...a lot alike."

"Oh, great. Thanks."

"Cassie, if the whole thing is as regimented as you make out, she can obviously tell when you're there and when you're not. What if turning up like that was her way of trying to reach out?"

"She still views me as...as..."

Lori reaches out and rests her hand on mine, bringing me to silence. "Maybe part of her does. Or maybe she finds it hard to let go. You get *that*, right?"

My eyes have glazed over a little, so I take a deep breath and calm myself down. "She blamed me for his death, and she intentionally made it impossible to live with her. I will *not* take the first step in this, and I'm not gonna back down on that. If *she* wants to try having a relationship with me again, *she* can come to me and *not* call me a murderer."

Lori smiles sadly. "Okay. Fair enough."

"You *really* don't want to sign this, do you?" I ask, sliding the tablet back toward me.

"No, I don't. It feels too much like signing your death warrant."

"I get what you mean, but..."

"And that feels too much like...like something Eddie must have done for himself."

And there it is. Her worry for me is genuine, I'm certain of that, but the comparison to her brother is a big part of it too. Maybe if I hadn't been the one to investigate Eddie's death and prove he'd hired the city's number one assassin, Devin Carmichael, to help him kill himself, this wouldn't be as hard for her. *But then you wouldn't have met her, and so this conversation wouldn't be happening anyway.*

I nod, switch the tablet to standby, and slip it back into my bag. "Okay."

"I'm sorry," Lori says, her eyes down.

"There's nothing to apologize for."

She looks up. "You're not angry?"

Now I reach out and give *her* hand a squeeze. "Don't be stupid. I may be stubborn, but I'm not going to throw a tantrum over not getting my own way. If you really don't want to do it, I'll just ask someone else. Like I said, it's not gonna be needed anyway, so what does it matter whose name goes on there?"

Lori lets out a sigh of relief. "Still," she says, lifting my hand and giving it a quick kiss. "I *am* glad you thought of me first."

"YA KNOW, I'M surprised. This time last year, you'd have taken her refusal as a sign you were already doomed."

I relax back into Devin's overly comfortable couch and offer a shrug. "This time last year, I wouldn't have been dating. Besides, I get what she means. Signing the will *would* have meant accepting there's a chance I could bite off more than I can chew with this one."

Devin pours a whiskey for himself and smiles. "Since when did *anything* ever stop you going too deep into something? If she thinks that'll stop you, she don't know you as well as she thinks."

I let out a short laugh and reply, "She's not an idiot, Devin. If she doesn't sign the thing, it means she doesn't have to think about it so much. Given what happened to her brother, I can't say I blame her for wanting some distance. Plus, maybe it felt too much like I was moving things forward too quickly. I mean, it's not as if we live together or anything."

"See, now those are the two things I don't wanna talk about, your love life and your lover's brother."

I wave the conversation away with a flick of my hand and say, "That's probably a good thing. I dread to think what advice you'd give if you were a relationship counsellor."

"There ain't no marital strife that can't be solved with a bullet to the head, darlin'." Devin swishes his drink in the glass and his face takes on a mischievous quality I'm pretty sure I'm not gonna enjoy. "Okay then, let's play a game. You want me to sign the will, then how about you tell me your thought process in coming to me. I clearly wasn't your first choice, but I bet I weren't your second either, was I?"

"There's no point me lying about that, is there?"

"Nope."

Play along, Cassie. It's easier to just go with it and give him what he wants to get what you want. Plus, he may not be willing to say you're his friend, but he is yours, and friendships are give-and-take.

I sigh. "Fine. No, you weren't number two on my list."

"I figured as much. So, who was?"

"Charlie."

Devin lets loose a full belly laugh. "You couldn't get your partner to sign, so you went crawling back to your ex?"

"No, I didn't go crawling back to her. I *considered* asking her, but...it felt inappropriate, okay? I'm with Lori. And Charlie's engaged."

"Inappropriate, huh? Well, that's one way to put it. Did you consider the police too? Maybe one of the team from the LV case?"

"I did, but I realized I wanted something a little extra from this, and they wouldn't be the right way to go with it. Well, *maybe* Donal, but I don't really know him well enough to ask."

"Well, now I'm intrigued. So, why me?"

I groan. "Because, as much as I was honest with Lori when I said I doubt anything would happen to me, she's right to worry. At least one thing about the case makes it a real possibility I'm gonna end up in a shitty situation, depending on the perpetrator's reason for going after my client. I'm malicious when I want to be. *If* the worst should happen, I want you to take what you need from my account, find the person responsible, and take them out."

"That seems like an extreme reaction, even for you."

"Maybe. I know Lori would want them to be brought to justice in such a scenario, but if things head the way that would make it most likely to play out, then there's the possibility they'd be untouchable by normal means. When normal doesn't work in New Hopeland, you either come to someone like me or someone like you. And I can't come to myself if I'm dead. Which means I'd need someone else to give her closure."

"It's funny, but as much as I keep my ear to the ground, *you* always manage to find something I didn't know about. This is sounding like one of *those* moments. Still. I like that. It keeps things interesting. Sure, I'll do it. And I'll even make sure Miss Redwood gets the rest of your stuff afterward."

I nod in agreement. "Thanks, Devin."

Devin tips his cowboy hat my way and smiles. "No problem, darlin'."

Chapter Two

"I APOLOGIZE FOR my silence in the car," Dr. Faraday says as she opens the door to her apartment.

"It's fine," I reply, shutting the door behind us. "It looked like you were working."

"Yes. Technically the job was completed during the day, but the team asked me to look over it for them. They're fairly new. Competent, but lacking in confidence in their abilities. Ordinarily, I'd do it once I was home, but the car journey afforded me time to glance over their work. I presumed you'd want to talk, too, so I thought I should take advantage of the opportunity."

"You're right that we *do* need to talk, but I would have been fine with you working. I know it isn't a long journey by car, but there was no need to rush what you needed to do."

"Oh, I didn't. It's not the first time my team has asked for input. I know where they're likely to make mistakes, and as is often the case, they don't appear to have. Like I said, they lack confidence, not skill."

I watch Dr. Faraday relax onto the couch, and lean myself against the wall opposite, crossing my arms. Contrary to popular belief, this is a genuinely relaxed pose for me, at least when I'm at work.

"Okay, let's get the standard stuff out of the way. I went through what you sent me on the Case Tool. You've given me plenty of detail to work with, so thank you for that. My plan is to start investigating the scene of individual incidents tomorrow. If anything additional springs to mind in the interim, tell me so I can make a note."

"I can certainly do that. Why tomorrow, though?"

"For a number of reasons. First, the initial paperwork took me a little longer than I expected. Second, it gives me time to consider if I need any other information from you. And third, I want to give anyone watching right now a clear message that I'm here to protect you before I start digging."

Dr. Faraday's eyes drift toward one of the ceiling cameras and she repeats, "Anyone watching?"

"Do you know what a ping box is?" Faraday glances back to me and nods. "I ran one in here earlier and gathered the details of all the outgoing signals. The destinations were the building servers, Familiar Enterprises, your ISP, and the local government security system. Given the stalker has been able to follow your movements so easily, I wouldn't have been surprised to find something unusual, or at least masked, among the signals. On the face of it, there's nothing unexpected in there. *If* there's someone monitoring you from inside, it leaves a couple of possibilities. The stalker could be using older tech the box isn't configured to find. Or the person watching you is either in the building or working at Familiar Enterprises."

"That's *if* someone is watching me at home."

I shrug. "Sure. But if they aren't, then they're definitely watching you somewhere. Which means we still can't rule out a fellow tenant or work colleague. You said in the Case Tool you couldn't think of anyone this may be. Is that still the case?"

"Yes. Sorry."

I shake my head. "Don't worry about it. If someone springs to mind, let me know, but otherwise, I'm hoping we'll find a suspect when I start looking into the different places you mentioned. Until then, though, I suggest you relax and carry on like it's a normal evening. Leave the worrying to me."

Faraday thinks about this for a moment, then nods and says, "Okay. Do you mind if I move to the computer?"

"Not at all. Do whatever you'd normally do."

She rises to her feet and replies, "Feel free to watch whatever you want. There's food and drink in the kitchen."

I drop onto the couch and stretch my arms over the back, dropping my head forward to crack my neck out. Once I feel the satisfying click, I turn my head to look over my shoulder at my client, who is now powering up her desktop. "I meant to ask about the food and drink, actually. I noticed it earlier, but you don't need it yourself, do you?"

"No, I do not."

"Then why keep it here? Won't it go to waste?"

"Some of it, yes, which is why I try not to overbuy. I do have friends, you know. It's for their benefit."

I watch her open a few tabs in her Internet browser while I consider her response. "That surprises me. You don't strike me as being too social."

"No?" she replies, her eyes still on the screen.

"No. The way you talk. Your general attitude. They're not really what most people would find endearing. Honestly, you seem pretty cold to me most of the times I've spoken to you. When you showed me what you were, I kinda figured it was because you're not human."

Faraday stops typing and turns the chair to look at me. She studies me for a moment, then says, "I'm masking. You are correct that I do not always have a natural way of speaking, but honestly, it has more to do with...introspection, I suppose. Until I know someone well, I am not very good at relaxing around them."

"So, until you've analyzed them and figured out how best to behave around them, you mean?"

"Caz, you are intentionally drawing attention to my physical nature."

"Well, yeah. What you're saying is very robot."

"You are applying that logic because you already know what I am. If you did not, you'd probably see it for what it is. I'm shy, Caz. And I lack social graces. That is all. But I do care. For example, the reason I have not had much company recently is I didn't want to risk one of my friends getting hurt. Oh, and I also care about how others view me, so thank you for discounting me so wholly."

"Hey, I'm not discounting you at all, I just..."

"Know what I am. How can I put this? Think of Bert. You have gained a general acceptance that he can die. For that to apply, you would also need to acknowledge him as, on some level, being alive."

"That's...okay, I'll concede maybe I view him differently to you, but I know him better."

"Exactly. You also know he was built differently to most Familiar Units much the same as I was. Just as Bert had a set role to fulfil, so do I. I am built to be akin to what I rather suspect you would term to be *a real person*. I am human in nature complete with faults and limitations."

"So, you're what, then? The next step of our evolution?"

"No, more of an analogue. I am not designed to replace pure humanity but rather to exist alongside it."

"Well, what else makes you more human then? It sounds like you've got a lot of the negatives of the deal. That's pretty cruel."

Dr. Faraday sighs. "I have what I like to call potential hot points. There are things I'm built to enjoy, and I have the potential to learn with certain topics or presentation styles being more conducive to that end. But I get the fun of figuring out what those things are myself."

"Ah, so you don't know what your favorite things are going to be until you find them."

"Exactly. Just as you wouldn't have known how much you enjoy being grumpy and judgmental until you gave it a try."

I blink, and let her words sink in. A smile rises to my lips and I chuckle. "I like this side of you. Mind if I grab a beer?"

Faraday returns my smile, turns back to the computer, and says, "I already said you could."

Wandering into the kitchen, I shout back, "So, you're built to be human, and Bert's built to be a menace to our apartment. What about the other one?"

"Other one?"

I stop in the doorway to the kitchen and crack open a can of cheap import. "Yeah. You told me before there were three hybrid programmed Familiars in the real world. So, that's you, Bert, and one other. I was curious as to what the other one is built to be."

"I don't have a clue. It wasn't deemed to be information I needed to know."

"Really? You must be curious, though, eh?"

"Oh, very. But I know better than to snoop. I'm sure I'll find out eventually anyway."

I take a mouthful of the relaxation juice and walk back toward the couch. "Who knows? Maybe one day, we all will. Okay, I'm going to go over the stuff you gave me on the Case Tool. I'll probably ask for more information on different things as I go along. Is that okay?"

"Of course."

THE SMELL OF coffee wafts through the darkness, and I raise my hand to rub my eyes. I sit up just as the light starts to pour in through my fingers, and Dr. Faraday walks into view and places a steaming mug on the table in front of me. "Nothing happened, I take it?" I ask.

"No. It was a pretty quiet evening."

I nod. Faraday had suggested I sleep, and I agreed under the proviso she wake me if anything happened. It's a common request. Normally, I'd pull an all-nighter on cases like this, in case my client *can't* stay awake. I guess that's a plus point to being hired by a robot. Sleep is something she doesn't need to do every night.

I pull my phone out of my trousers and load up an app. "I remote summoned Bert, just in case. He's been stationed on the roof of the building all night. Looks like he didn't spot anything either."

"That is good. You won't want to leave him out there all day, though. We're due some rain, and there's always the chance it'll get in through his joints. It's only a one percent chance, but it's a chance all the same."

"Noted. It would be good to have him on hand here, but he can be a bit...destructive."

"Ah, yes. That shouldn't be a problem. Call him down to the balcony after breakfast and I'll show you why."

"Breakfast, huh?" I yawn, then take a mouthful of my drink. It's a strong blend, but there's something else drifting in over the top of it now. I take a sniff and my head instinctively turns toward the kitchen.

"Pancakes and bacon," Dr. Faraday clarifies as she heads back to the kitchen. She returns with a plate of said items and adds, "And no, it's not because it's a stereotypical Canadian food. Quite aside from anything else, I don't have any maple syrup. I happened to notice the open pancakes and bacon on your kitchen side, so I thought it would be a good choice for breakfast."

"I'm going to have to start tidying up more. Thank you, though. I prefer them without the syrup anyway."

I pick up the knife and fork and start eating my client's morning offering. I must have looked pretty ravenous, because Faraday asks, "They're good, I take it?"

I nod. "Honestly, I'm not great at feeding myself in the morning. I normally stick with toast. Unless Lori's staying over. She's my partner. I kinda take extra steps then." I swallow a mouthful and continue. "Anyway, something's been bugging me. It hit me before I drifted off last night. Why did you come to me? All things considered I would have thought Jonah Burrell would have been able to offer you more than I can in terms of protection. Or if not him, then the police. Don't get me wrong, I'm happy to continue with the case, I'm just curious."

"If I'm being honest, I *did* consider both routes. However, Mr. Burrell is *not* a security person. He offers ample protection in the office as a standard, but he is under no obligation to provide the same in my home. As such, I have not yet made him aware of my situation."

"You haven't told him?"

"No. Unless it comes to affect my work, I didn't see any need. I am designed to blend in, and reporting something that has no bearing on your work to your boss is not normal behavior."

"Perhaps," I reply between bites. "But in that case, the police would have been the normal route."

"Agreed. But you've seen what I have in terms of evidence. There simply isn't enough for the police to be able to do too much."

"They'd do the same thing I am, though. A little slower maybe, and if it came down to it, they'd likely use different information sources, but they'd follow the same core procedures."

"I'm not so sure. I read a few reports recently that the police only solve a little over three percent of cases such as this before harm comes to the victim. In the majority, either no arrests are made prior to harm occurring, or the victim is already hurt, in which case they can't really ignore it. Most people have better results going private. PIs tend to take these things far more seriously and can dedicate much more time to the case as a single focus, rather than dealing with multiple cases at once. When it comes to local investigators, you are the most highly regarded in the city. That you know what I am also helps."

"I appreciate the faith, but still. That's a low figure. What reports were they? Or which sites?"

"I'd have to look up the names now. They weren't on any of the mainstream sites; I don't trust those so much. And they were primarily anecdotal in nature."

I pause, thinking back to the conversations I had with Dr. Faraday during the LV incident. "Unusual news site and genetic mutations...you're a conspiracy theorist."

"I prefer truth hunter, as cheesy as it sounds, but yes."

"Is that what you were doing last night then? Trawling conspiracy sites?"

"Yes."

I consider making a comment about there being a reason no conspiracy theories are ever proven to be correct but think better of it. I spend my free time watching films I know are going to give me sleepless nights, so it's not like I don't have ridiculous hobbies. "Fair enough. So, how about you show me this trick with Bert?"

"Ah, yes. If you could summon him, I'll grab something from the kitchen."

I reopen the app on my phone and call Bert to the balcony. He waits patiently until Dr. Faraday returns and opens the door for him, then waddles in and starts looking around. "Now," Faraday explains, "most Familiars are programmed to not misbehave in other people's homes. While Bert is no exception to this rule, his hybrid programming certainly leaves the option to do so open. However, there is a distraction technique that should nullify it."

She pulls a small dome-shaped item from her pocket and places it on the floor in front of her, then steps back and signals me to watch. After a moment, Bert stops what he's doing—from his head movements and claw flexes, I think he may have been planning the best way to climb the walls—and turns toward the dome. He walks over to investigate and reaches out to touch it but stops just short of doing so. He pauses to look at the dome, says, "Caw," and wanders off again.

"It scans his behavioral data in real time," Dr. Faraday explains. "When it detects a potentially negative action, it starts sending out signals to draw his attention, then gives him a mild stimulus when he comes close. It's a very basic system, but it's proven effective with various different Familiar Units."

"Huh. Won't he grow wise to it, though?"

"It'll change up the signals to avoid boredom, and the stimulus is pleasant for him, so that's unlikely. I could probably *acquire* a spare for you at home if it would be of help?"

I wave the suggestion away with my fork and eat the last piece of pancake on my plate. "Thanks, but there's no need. I like his little eccentricities. If it means a tidy-up once in a while, that's fine. Though it would be useful for when I have to take him to other locations for prolonged periods."

"I shall see what I can find."

"Thanks," I say, rising to my feet and downing my now cool coffee. "Right. I'm gonna get a wash, then I'll drive you to work and start gathering security cam footage. If something happens before I'm done, try to give me a shout as quickly as you can. Bert's too efficient for his own good, and I'd like there to be enough left of the culprit to question."

THE PROBLEM WITH having a car is you get used to using it. Not to mention sometimes it's a requirement that leaves you in an awkward position. Now I've driven Dr. Faraday to work, I've realized something important. "I need to do a walk through before I start collecting footage," I reiterate to myself.

Which leaves me in the position of needing to *not* use the car for a moment but not being sure where to leave it. *Well, security is looking at me, so I may as well start there.*

I wave the curious security guard over and put on my best I'm-really-nice-and-just-trying-to-get-my-own-way voice. "Hi. Quick question. The public parking lot is for customers only, isn't it?"

He nods. "Yeah. You a customer?"

"Sort of. I mean, I do have a Familiar, and I do come by for the regular checks. Today specifically, though, I was dropping a friend in. Dr. Faraday. Do you know her?"

"Of course," he replies, his face lighting up into a smile. "Nice lady. Lots of interesting ideas about the city."

"Yeah?" I shake my head, dismissing my natural urge to get sidetracked. "Sorry. So yeah, I was dropping her in today, and I'll be picking her up again later too. The thing is, I have a couple of errands to run, so since I was delivering staff and am *technically* a customer, I was wondering if I could maybe use the parking lot?"

The security guard sighs, and it becomes clear he gets asked things like this a lot. "Seeing as you're technically a customer, you could. Since you're not technically a customer today, though, I'd also technically have to have your car towed the second you leave the premises."

"Seriously?"

"Afraid so. Look, I'd love to help you, but Mr. Burrell is really strict with this sort of thing."

Well, at least he's not just being obstructive for no reason. "No, no, it's fine. I was trying my luck anyway, eh."

"Sorry about that."

"Don't worry about it. I can find another spot, I'm sure."

"Okay. Good, I guess."

The silence hangs awkwardly for a moment. Looks like someone's bad at goodbyes today. *And he's not much better*, I tease myself. Rather than draw things out more than I need to, I simply start the car, give a polite wave, and pull out.

I head back to Faraday's apartment block. I arrive swiftly. The next step is to load up the interactive map on my tablet. I don't use the feature too often, largely because it had a habit of crashing the machine before Lori helped get the thing tuned up, but it fits well with this case. Dr. Faraday's movements are identical every day with the one exception of the final meeting with her stalker, so I was able to plot out her route with a nice visual aid last night. I should also be able to mark what cameras I'll likely need footage from on the app and let it auto synch with my case notes, which will make things a little easier.

Even though the apartment is only six blocks from the FE Limited offices, the first walk-through takes me a little while. The area is home to a good amount of businesses, so there are plenty of security cameras around, and that's before I even take the local government ones into account. The good thing is, as they're not only all in different places, but at different heights, there are two store cameras and one government camera with decent visibility that should have caught sight of Faraday on her way into work during the first third of the journey. Then there's another one attached to a shop a little further on, another government cam, and finally the FE Limited external cameras *if* I need them. I'll leave the FE ones for now, as Faraday requested I not draw too much attention to the case for her. If it comes down to it, it's good to know they're there, though.

Walk-through number two is the normal return route. Which is the same as the initial route, but in reverse. I could have checked the cameras for both sides of the journey during the first trip, but concentrating on the cameras from one standpoint at a time is the better way to do it in my opinion. I can ensure my focus is squarely on this part of the journey and avoid missing anything by trying to check too much at once.

That and you want to color-code the notes and not have to switch back and forth as you go.

I add another five assorted cameras to the list and walk back a few blocks for the third and final walk-through. This, I'm certain, will be the important one as this takes me along the alternate route and up to where the actual meeting took place. Sure enough, right where the stalker is supposed to have stopped, there's a security camera just above the back door to...somewhere. A quick check around the other side of the alley shows, to my surprise, it's a residential property.

"Okay, so I've got eleven cameras I definitely want to review. Let's get this sorted." I pull my cell phone out and call through to the station.

"New Hopeland PD."

"Hi, this is Cassie Tam. Look, I'm working a case, and Captain Hoover signed off on the papers for it earlier. Is he available at all?"

"He's in a meeting, I'm afraid. Would you like him to call you back? Or I could pass on a message."

"Uh...maybe. Is Lieutenant Hanson there? Or Corporal Devereaux, maybe?"

"I'll just check." The phone goes quiet, and after a moment, his voice returns. "Corporal Devereaux is available. Should I pass you through?"

"Yes, please."

"One moment."

The line goes quiet for long enough I start to think I've been cut off. Thankfully, the next sound I hear is a click, followed by the familiar voice of William Devereaux. "Hi, Tam. How's the car?"

"She's great, Will. How about you? Hanson hasn't driven you off the force yet?"

He laughs. "Nah, I'm far too set on getting to the same rank as her. She can't boss me around too much then, eh."

"Somehow, I doubt it would stop her."

"True. So, what can I do for you? This something to do with the stalker case?"

I frown. "How'd you know that? It's not like Hoove to go around talking about things too openly."

"He didn't. I got bored, so when I saw he'd been meeting with you, I had a quick look on the system."

I roll my eyes and smile to myself. "You want to be careful or you'll sabotage the promotion you're ever-so-subtly chasing. But yeah, it's about that. I'm gonna be putting in some warrant requests in a minute and wanted to see if someone could keep an eye out for them and get them signed off quickly."

"Sure. You don't want delays when you're dealing with a stalker. How many will there be?"

"Eleven. All for CCTV footage."

Devereaux whistles down the receiver, giving away what he thinks of the number. To be extra certain he's been clear, he comments, "That's a lot."

"Good job they're the simple version of the forms, eh?" I reply, not taking the bait.

He laughs. "It does make it simpler at our end, in fairness. With you, I don't think most people check them too thoroughly now. Actually, scratch that. The last time you sent some across, Hoove gave them to someone to check through as a training exercise."

"Huh. Explains why *that* took so long."

"Take it as a compliment. He figured they'd be a good example of a correctly completed form. Easy for the first timer to check, and it gives them a name to look out for."

"And there's me thinking I was only ever a *bad* example. Anyway, I better get the forms done. Thanks for this, Will. Say hi to Hanson for me."

"She's not been well today, so I'll have to pass it on when I see her. I may check in with her later, so no problem there. Catch you later, Tam."

The line goes dead, and I can't help but smile. Given how bad a foot we got off on when we first met, Will has really softened around me the last few months. After the LV case, he's been even more relaxed. Whether it's trust gained through working collaboratively with me or just that dating Hanson has mellowed him a bit, I don't know. I'll assume it's the work. If the stories Hanson herself tells are to be believed, she is a nightmarish partner.

"Right, enough stalling. Paperwork."

THE KETTLE GIVES a satisfying click, and I pour the boiling water in on top of the instant coffee and milk. Dr. Faraday did say I could help myself, after all.

Gathering the footage was as mundane as it ever was, with all the usual steps falling into place. *Hi there, here's a warrant. No, you're not in trouble, I just need to access your cameras. Oh, there was a crime, and I'm investigating. Don't worry, I'll only take what I need.* Those were the public cameras anyway. The local government Key Building cameras were a healthy mix of intrusive staff and snarky backchat.

I walk into the living room area and place my mug down on the table. Bert is happily exploring the room a little, with occasional stops at the distraction toy Dr. Faraday set up for him. She also showed me a trick I wasn't aware of. All modern TVs can synch up with other electronic devices, which means the footage I downloaded to my servers can be *cast* onto the big screen in front of me. I can even still control it on the tablet. Which is really useful.

I decide to start with the final piece of footage. I didn't bother checking the rest of it too much when I gathered it, other than to confirm Dr. Faraday was on screen. Until I could view this clip properly, I wouldn't know who else to look for. What's more, the homeowner was about as nosy as you can be without coming across as rude, so I took the same approach when I downloaded this chunk. I do want to afford my client *some* privacy if I can. So, this will be my first time seeing the perpetrator. *If* they were caught on the camera.

The video starts with a shot of the empty alley, but within seconds, Dr. Faraday walks by. Her face interests me. Her eyes are a little wide, and her pupils are dilated. There's a tenseness in her shoulders, and her pace is relatively brisk. Of course, those are natural responses to what's happening, but it's amazing how much attention to detail Jonah paid with her on such a microscopic level. For all intents and purposes, she appears to be as human as I am. "Incredible," I murmur.

Just as Dr. Faraday exits the right side of the screen, another figure wanders into view. They're wearing a pair of nondescript jeans. I can tell they're cheap because they look immaculate, almost certainly new, but the current batch being stocked by the high-end shops are all covered in heavy logo branding or patterns. These are plain, old school blue. The person is also wearing a plain black hoodie. Just like the Doc said, it's baggy enough to hide their shape, and the hood is up. Even before they turn to face the camera, I notice something is most definitely wrong. I can't see their face at all, because it's been covered in solid black. Sure enough, when they turn to face the camera, the mass of color instantly expands to cover the entire area beneath the hood.

"Huh. That's strange. It didn't censor Faraday's face at all."

The person continues to stare at the camera. Eventually, they turn and head back the way they came. The video ends and I sit back on the couch to think things through. *Okay, first things first. The camera owner gave me her number in case I needed anything else. Let's start there.*

A few quick taps on the screen of my cell phone gives way to three quiet rings, followed by a soft, "Hello?"

"Hi. This is Cassie Tam. We spoke earlier. Mrs. Bush, right?"

"Oh, the detective. Was the footage okay? Did it help at all?"

"Sort of. Listen, can you access it yourself?"

"I'm at the computer, so I don't see why not. Why's that?"

"The copy I have shows what I wanted, but the face of the person I'm trying to catch is censored for some reason. I was wondering if it was the same on the source file or if it was just an error at my end."

"Really? Well that's unusual; I don't use any masking software. Hold on, I'll call up the video."

"Thank you. Do you need the time stamp?"

"No, no, I remember...ah, here we go. So...there goes...oh. I see what you mean. The person with the hood up, are they the one you mean?"

"Yeah, that's them."

"Well, I mean, the camera would likely pick up some shadow back there, but this isn't that, obviously. I'm sorry, but I don't know what to tell you. It's just...quite concerning, is all."

"Is there any chance it was a setting you can, I don't know, reverse?"

"No, like I said, no masking software. I'll have to run a full diagnostic on the system to see if something got in. It's strange how it managed to cover that one person so perfectly, though."

"I thought so too. Okay, in that case, I'm sorry to bother you again. If you find anything on your system, could you give me a call?"

"Of course."

"Thank you, Mrs. Bush. If I come across the solution, I'll do the same. In the meantime, I hope you can fix any problems you might discover."

"Me too. Good luck, detective."

Mrs. Bush hangs up, and I restart the video. This time, I zoom in on the censored face of the stalker. Interestingly, on the big screen, I can see the black mark isn't entirely solid. It's moving. Zooming closer shows this mass, unfortunately, isn't mapped to the stalker's facial structure. Instead, a slightly lighter shade of darkness is constantly swirling around the solid layer. "It's like a living version of my ties."

There. A slight twitch in the shoulder. On the small screen, I would have missed it. I rewind the video a little and move the zoomed image down the arm and pause the footage. Frowning, I set a short section to play on an isolated loop. The movements are subtle, but the person is definitely moving their fingers while they're staring at the camera. It looks like the tips of their fingers—or to be more precise, the tips of their glove—are glowing too.

Good job. Alleys tend to be darker, or that would have definitely passed me by. I wonder if Dr. Faraday would be interested in giving me the TV?

I run through the video again to add some visual marks and annotations, then save the modified file.

"Okay, let's see what else we've got."

I load up the next video and set it to run at half speed. Once I spot Dr. Faraday, I start scanning around the screen and eventually find the hooded figure in the background, following along behind her. Once again, their face is censored by the swirling black mass. In another video, they're standing still on the corner, just watching my client walk by. In another, they're sticking close but not quite within touching distance. Every single video is the same. They're there, in plain sight, and their face is hidden. I mark their location anyway.

"The video where they're staring at the camera is the important one. The others they must have planned through observation, because they're just ignoring the cameras. Whatever they've done, they'd already done it before they started playing chase. The change in route Dr. Faraday took combined with their reaction means they hadn't pre-planned being caught on that one. So, what were they doing?"

I swallow a mouthful of slightly cold coffee and sigh. "Think, Cassie. It has to be software based, so maybe it takes a little while to set up, or they were worried about whatever they're using being spotted if they installed it in too many places? If we're working on the theory they only had it set up where they knew they'd need it, that means it acts retroactively on the video files, censoring just *their* face. That's a pretty specific task. I guess I could run a search to see if there's something online.

"Still, the gloves are fairly easy to figure out if it *is* true. The LV's gloves were linked to their masks, allowing them to control their gear. You can buy similar in most computer stores now. These will probably be hooked up to a tablet or maybe even contact lenses. They're noting the location of the camera. so they can make sure they're not spotted.

"Okay, let's chase that. First, though..."

I hit the voice command button on my tablet and say, "Open server six, open case files, sub-folder Faraday. Create new sub-folder titled Annotated Files. Move videos from tablet to Annotated Files."

Without a link to my home speaker system here, the tablet is in silent mode, so it works the actions without noise. Once the screen confirms the files have been moved, I access them manually to make sure the process is actually finished. Once I'm satisfied, I draft up a report for the main Governmental Monitoring Office. In part, that's because I'm a good girl, but I legally have to do it now I've found a potential breach of a governmental system. Mostly, it's because knowing the main GMO will look into it rather than the Key Building means if they find anything useful, then it'll likely be someone I've at least worked with before controlling the case. That increases the likelihood of them passing the information to me, or at least the useful bits.

"Right. More coffee, then I hit the Internet. Maybe I'll find something that can at least unscramble the video."

"Caw," Bert agrees.

Chapter Three

THE INTERNET IS a vast and incredibly useful place. There are all manner of free tools available now, a lot of which are on par with the more expensive products you can buy, especially when it comes to picture and video manipulation. The best part is, in this wireless age, most of the tools are online and don't require you to download anything, you just need to upload the file you want checked. Which, given my tablet's already stuffed memory card, is a very good thing.

Of course, client confidentiality being what it is, I have to be selective in what tools I use. Not to mention which clips. In this instance, I decide to go for what *should* give me the highest chance of getting some results: a cut down three-second clip of the stalker staring at the camera, and a still from the same video. It's short, so uploading doesn't take long, the quality is surprisingly high, and there's nothing on the footage other than the person I want to catch.

NO EDITING DETECTED.

I groan. "Looks like the still is a no go then. At least with what I have available. I guess that makes sense. The video was edited, so I'm really just taking a screen shot of the postproduction with it. Okay, let's try the video itself."

The first two sites I upload the video to come up with similar results. They were designed to look for very basic things, so all that means is whatever's being used isn't particularly basic at its core. Even if they hadn't been able to remove the effect, they'd have detected something was there if it had been a modification of anything else.

Which means we need to roll out the big guns.

I switch on my limited use Virtual Private Network, or VPN, and navigate to what I like to call a "buried site." It's not exactly on the dark web, but it's well hidden, and you certainly don't want to be tracked by anyone on there. Not unless you *like* removing viruses from your machines anyway. The site does have a decent video suite, though. I only venture in here when I need to, as I'm not even close to being into file modding, but it hasn't stopped anyone from helping me yet. Probably because the stuff I bring here is interesting to them.

My username here is DirtGrabShriekBlast. I was genuinely surprised when my fellow surfers figured out what movie franchise I was referencing so quickly. Clearly, I'm not the last monster fan left standing out there. They were technically right that the last part should have read Ass rather than Blast if I followed the pattern, but I couldn't bring myself to refer to myself as Ass. Even if it *does* fit, sometimes.

My file uploads quickly, and a message flashes up on screen.

PLEASE COMPLETE THE FOLLOWING BOXES: TIME LIMIT AND REASON FOR UPLOAD.

This is where the site comes into its own. Everything you upload is set with an expiry date and is automatically made available to the people online. It's an active community, by which I mean the people frequenting the site are inactive in reality and like to mess around with whatever comes their way on here. One of the members, Dented_03, once told me it was just a way to pass the time while they traded crypto currency and shares. Who'd have thought the web dwellers were so money savvy, eh?

The time limit is in minutes, so I enter "30" and add "need to uncover face" as the reason, then head into the video tool. It gives the clip a couple of scans and fails to find anything on there. The third, deeper scan finds evidence of tampering and sets about trying to remove it. To my surprise, it comes back quite quickly with a message reading *MASKING REMOVED*. Less surprising is the fact the *fixed* video is no different to the pre-edited one.

I drum my fingers on the table. *Guess I'll leave it to the community for now. Let's give the PD a try while I wait.*

I call through to the station and a familiar voice from earlier cuts in. "New Hopeland PD."

"Hi, this is Cassie Tam. Can you put me through to Corporal Devereaux? He was helping me earlier, and I wanted to update him."

"Ah, yes, I remember. Sure, I'll pass you through now."

The phone clicks and I start, "Will, it's Cassie. Quick question..."

"Oh, hi Cassie," Lieutenant Hanson answers. "How are you?"

"I'm fine," I reply, and my brow furrows. "Aren't you supposed to be off sick?"

She yawns. "I'm tired more than anything. I haven't been sleeping too well."

"Huh. How come?"

"Because reasons. They're sending me home again in a minute, anyway. I'm just guarding Dev's desk while he gets ready to play escort for me. You said you had a question?"

"Yeah, but if you're not at your desk, I'm not sure you'll be able to answer it."

"It's a current caseload thing then, yeah? Don't worry, Dev forgot to lock his screen. I was just changing his wallpaper to some sort of large snake. I'm not sure what it is other than big."

"Okay...why?"

"He has ophidiophobia. I'm using flooding to help him get over it."

I chuckle. "No, you're trying to cheer yourself up. You're looking forward to his reaction when he gets back there after taking you home and logs back in."

"That too. Anyway, what's the question?"

"I'm working a stalker case. It turns out the culprit has found a way to mask their face on camera, and what they've used is definitely not a conventional piece of software. It looks like it masks old files automatically. I wanted to know if anything had come up recently."

"Bit of a weird topic, but I'll run a keyword search. Hold on."

I hear Hanson typing away in the background, and someone walks up and starts speaking to her. My name is mentioned, and Corporal Devereaux comes onto the line. "Hi, Tam. Sorry about Hanson, she's just being ridiculously uncompliant with the whole 'staying home from work' thing."

"I'm fine," she says just loud enough for me to hear over the phone.

"In fairness, Will, she does sound pretty much like herself. Aside from the yawning."

"Yeah, but you can't *see* her."

There's a clattering, and Hanson comes back on the line. "I'll get him for that one. Panda eyes are in, anyway.

Okay, I've run searches for censorship, masking, editing, video cameras, and software. There's some theft, but nothing that sounds like what you described."

"Which means one of three things: nobody's come forward with a report yet, it's something entirely new, or it's something new to the city."

"Exactly."

"Okay, well that at least tells me I need to dig deeper."

"Which is something new for you, right?"

I laugh. "Thanks, Hanson. You better get home though, eh?"

She sighs. "I suppose. If I was dumb enough to let Dev *snake* his way into my affections, I suppose I should let him play the knight in shining armor once in a while, right? Or cab driver in a uniform at least."

"I think you may owe him that. Did you manage to change the wallpaper?"

"Yup."

"Well, have fun with that."

"And you with this," Hanson replies. "Catch you later."

She hangs up, and I smile. "I really do feel sorry for you, Will."

Back onto the more useful dark corners of the web and my video has gotten some attention. By which I mean it has a fair number of registered downloads. No comments, but that's understandable. This lot are mostly silent unless they have something to actually add to the conversation. If there are no comments, then it means nobody has found anything worth mentioning publicly. I do have one pending request, though; a voice chat request from Xx^_^xX.

"Who needs names when you can use symbols. Wasn't there a musician who did that?" I mumble, synching my phone up to the tablet and adding a standard voice mask. Once it's all set up, I hit accept on the request and wait for Xx^_^xX to stop whatever they're doing and take the call. When they do accept, the voice coming out of my phone is borderline robotic.

"Hey. I have to ask; did you do the video yourself?"

"Afraid not," I reply. "I wouldn't have posted for help if I had."

"You're not a regular poster, so I guess you wouldn't know, but we do get plenty of things like that. Mostly people using the site as a testing ground. If it takes us more than ten minutes to figure it out, it's probably good enough for general public use, that's the thinking. So, if you're not responsible, this is of personal interest for non-software-business purposes, right?"

I snort. "You know full well I'm not going to confirm or deny that. This place is supposed to be great for anonymity."

"Sure, I was just being curious. Anyway, the video is interesting. I ran it through a virtual system a couple of times, and do you know what I found?"

"No, what?"

"Fuck all. It's clear the video has been tampered with, but nothing *I* own can unscramble it. That's odd, because I can usually get rid of most censorship marks."

"So, do you have any idea what could be doing it?"

"Software."

"Obviously it's software. I mean what kind?"

"Very clever software. And I'll tell you why. After the first couple of times I played with it, I was near convinced the person's face must have really looked that way. Even when I was getting confirmation my system had removed censorship, it looked no different. There was nothing there to unscramble because for all intents and purposes, nothing had been scrambled, that's what it seemed like. But on the fifth time I noticed something."

They pause. I wait for a moment, then give them what they clearly want. "Okay, so what did you notice?"

"For a moment, when the file first opens, there's a jump in disk space used."

"So, there was something attached to the video? That's...my scans didn't pick anything up. *Diu.* That means my servers are infected."

"Well, I have some good news for you. While you're probably right that anywhere you stored the file is infected, it's most likely pretty harmless. There is no indication it does anything other than create the visual effect. And even then, I think it needs some specific triggers."

"Okay, what makes you think that?"

"Well, I tried running a few other videos through the virtual system after the one you uploaded. The files grew in size a little, meaning whatever you uploaded *did* take effect, but it didn't censor any faces in there."

"Which means something on the person's face must cause it to activate."

"Exactly. Now, this is from a pretty good camera, but given how the censorship thing spreads, I'm willing to bet two things. First, it works both retroactively and in real time, and second, it would work just fine on lower end cameras too. If I'm right about the second one, it must mean it isn't using a complex facial scanning system."

"So, it's got to be what? A mask? No, that can't be right. Someone would have reacted."

"And profession confirmed. You're a detective."

I frown. There's no real need to hide it. "I am. What gave it away?"

"Well, if you weren't the creator, then that means you had to have a reason for having the footage. It was pretty creepy, to be fair, so my first thought was maybe it was a burglar who broke in somewhere. You weren't reacting to the conversation like a victim, which meant you were on the other end of the scale in terms of the good guys. Official law enforcement doesn't tend to visit our humble abode, so you'd have to be private. You said someone would have reacted, which means you have more than one video, and at least some of them are in more public areas than this one. So, it has to be a crime you're trying to solve, and you're not with the police. Don't worry, I follow the rules. What's said in the chat stays in the chat."

"Good to know. Any ideas what the trigger may be?"

"Oh, I agree with you, it'll be a mask. You heard of T1Stretch?"

"No."

"It's a material designed to sit snug on the face, forming to the shape of the wearer. If the coloring is right, it's virtually unnoticeable. These masks are designed to be used as a confidence builder for victims of severe facial injuries. Since the success of the initial application as a specialist psychological tool, though, there are semi-commercially available versions. The difference is the buyable ones are transparent by default. They get used for special effects mostly."

"I think I see where you're going with this. If the person wore a transparent one it would explain nobody noticing it."

"Exactly. All they'd need then is for there to be a marker on it, maybe a specific tinting or something like that, the cameras would pick up. That activates the software, and, at a guess, it alters how the camera registers certain colors, leading to the censored videos."

"The tinting, if that's what it is, would need to be natural looking enough not to be noticeable, but not so real the software censors everyone. Wearing their hood up probably helps with that."

"That sounds about right. Do you know what the cleverest part of the software is, though? After the initial disk space jump, everything goes back to normal. It modifies what it needs to, then disappears. Even now, with the virtual screen open in front of me, I know the software's there, but I can't find it. It's near untraceable. I *will* find it, I'm sure, but unless you know to look for it, you won't even notice. Standard tools won't find it either, I'm certain. At a guess, I'm expecting to find it's deleted a bunch of junk files and hidden itself in their place."

"Huh. That all feels kinda overkill for what I'm working on."

Xx^_^xX laughs. "Well, that's about all I've got for you. The software won't get to my main system, so I'm going to have some fun trying to trace it. I hope that was a help, detective."

They hang up.

I sit back into the couch and cross my arms. "It may not be overkill if they *do* know what Dr. Faraday is."

"I APOLOGIZE," DR. Faraday says as she slides into the front passenger seat of the car. "I *did* instruct security to let you in if you should come by, but I hadn't realized there was to be a changing of the guards today. If I had, I would have ensured you didn't have to have an argument."

I wave her concerns away with a light flick of my wrist. "Don't worry about it. I've dealt with worse, not to mention grumpier, security guards before now. With some of them I've carried through with the threats."

"Yes, well, I wouldn't recommend it here. While I don't doubt starting a fist fight with Miss Lansdowne would give the office staff some evening entertainment, it would also make it rather difficult for me to gain you further access."

"Further access," I repeat, pulling out onto the main road. "What did you have in mind?"

"As it stands, I should be able to have you added to all the guards' safe entry lists. It should mean you're given general access to the building without issue. If that fails, I'll have some meeting slots set up, so you appear on record as an official customer visit."

"You know, you could just speak to Jonah and let him know what's going on. I'm sure he'd help sort out some 'general access' as you put it."

"As I said, Caz, I don't want to worry Mr. Burrell unless absolutely necessary."

I sigh. "Well, I can't fault you for conforming to social standards. Honestly, I've had plenty of clients take similar routes with their bosses, and near enough all of them ended up having to tell them in the end. You may do well to cut down on the time, and just skip ahead. You could look at it like an office project. I mean, you must have to deal with efficiencies, eh?"

"I will take it under consideration. You missed the turn, by the way."

"I know. I have a few things I need to do. I would have got it all done before coming to get you, but I had an interesting set of conversations with some helpful people. So, we're heading to my office. Once I'm done there, I can finish the rest up back at yours."

She nods. "Am I to assume you have made some headway with my case, then?"

"To a point. It's hard to explain without showing you a few things from the security footage I gathered, and I was stupid enough to leave my tablet at your place in my rush to pick you up. Sorry about that."

"No bother. Is Bert still there too?"

"Yeah. Just in case anyone tries breaking in."

"And the distraction toy is still working?"

I shrug. "Seemed to be. Bert being Bert, who can be sure? For all I know, we'll get back there and find he's redecorated the chairs with some edgy but oh so fashionable gnaw marks."

Dr. Faraday lets out a short, but all too human laugh, and her lips raise into a smile. "It's no wonder you're so attached to him. He's a real bundle of personality, isn't he?"

"He is that," I reply, pulling the car to a stop. "You better come in with me, just in case."

"Of course."

We enter the building, and I spot the resident handyman, Mr. Thorne, coming out of the elevator. He sees me and gives a cheery wave, then stops in the doorway to keep it open. "You're back," he says.

"Only briefly, I'm afraid. Mr. Thorne, this is Dr. Faraday. Dr. Faraday, Mr. Thorne. He does all the maintenance in the building."

"Unless it's overly complicated," he adds, offering a handshake. Dr. Faraday accepts it gratefully. "I hope there's nothing too serious happening to keep you away. I haven't seen or heard Bert either."

"Just another case," I say. "We're staying with Dr. Faraday until it's resolved. I can't say any more, I'm afraid."

"Fair enough. Knowing you, if it was that bad, it'd make the papers anyway."

I shake my head, but smile. "Don't I know it."

Mr. Thorne ushers us into the elevator, and we head up to my office. It *is* strangely quiet without Bert inside. If he'd been there and it was this quiet, I'd almost be expecting to find a mass of destruction complete with a mangled intruder waiting for me. Instead, it's empty.

"I won't be long," I say. "I just need Bert's charger, some extra clothes, and to set up some stuff to deter potential visitors."

Dr. Faraday nods and takes herself to the couch, where she sits and starts studying the room. I'd be offended if she were human, but this I'll put down to an analytical curiosity. Clothing wise, I snag another plain white shirt and trousers that match those I'm wearing. I also grab some fresh underwear because it's always worth having more than you need. The charger is resting on a shelf just outside the bedroom, so it's easy to find. Once I have the items packed into a bag, I take my cell phone out of my pocket and walk over to the security panel next to the front door.

I flip open a lower panel and press the phone to it, letting them synch up, and then type up a simple message on the screen: *I AM CURRENTLY WORKING A CASE AND CANNOT TAKE ON FURTHER CLIENTS UNTIL IT*

IS RESOLVED. I APOLOGIZE FOR THE INCONVENIENCE. IF YOUR CASE IS URGENT AND THE POLICE ARE NOT AN OPTION, I RECOMMEND CONTACTING GEOFF TARBY.

The message will project across the glass on the door if someone knocks and will come with a scannable code designed to put whoever sees it in contact with Geoff. He's a good man. Not as good at his job as I am, but he's decent. Plus, when he's away, he does me the courtesy of giving my details as a recommendation, so why shouldn't I return the favor? The message *should* synch up with my work number too, so that saves some time.

"Okay, let's get going," I say and open the door. Dr. Faraday joins me, and we make our way back to the car. The traffic is clear enough that we make it back to Dr. Faraday's place fairly quickly, too, reducing the need for awkward small talk. Which is nice. Once we're inside and have checked Bert is behaving himself, it's down to business.

I load up the security video where the stalker looks directly at the camera and let Faraday watch it through. Afterwards, I show her some stills from the other videos. She frowns. "Can the images be unscrambled?"

"That's what I wanted to know. So, after checking there hadn't been anything similar reported to the police—there hadn't, by the way—I had the footage looked at by some associates online."

"Trustworthy associates, I assume?"

I shrug. "As they can be. They're the sort of people who have an interest in this sort of stuff, and the site lets me limit how much access is given to the files and for how long. Don't worry, you weren't in what I sent them."

"I see. And did they manage to clean the footage?"

"No. It isn't so much that the footage has been censored, something was sent to the cameras and forced them to pick up certain things differently. It's sort of like if someone had a genetic quirk that meant certain shades of color were undecipherable to their brain, I guess. The file spreads with the footage though, so...*diu.*"

"What's wrong?"

"I cast it to your TV. It will have spread to anything else that synchs up with it. Does that include your computer?"

She shakes her head. "No. It will include the security camera, though. Is whatever it is dangerous?"

"As far as I can tell, it only affects the way this person translates into an image. My working theory is they're wearing a mask with a set color or pattern on it, and that's what's being targeted by the software. It'd have to be a realistic looking thing, or people would have noticed them. From what I've seen, they seem to have blended in with the crowd pretty well. Anyway, sorry. I didn't realize."

"It's fine, I'm sure. I can get the machines cleaned easily enough."

"Good. How soon, actually? If the person comes here, maybe they'll be expecting the software to be installed, and we can catch them by surprise?"

"Unfortunately, I can't do a system restore myself. I'll contact the tech support team for the television and speak to the building attendant for the camera. Based on experience, we're looking at a day at least."

"Okay, that's not too long. I tell you what, I need to make a quick call myself. Why don't you get onto them, and I'll see if I can find out anything else."

Faraday nods and walks over to her computer chair. She sits and pulls out her cell phone. I do the same and hit the speed dial for Lori. After a few rings, she picks up with a cheery, "Hi, Cassie."

"Hey, Lori. How's your day been?"

"Um…frustrating. And still not over. We had a bunch of errors with the computers and everyone is scrambling to restore backups and rework pieces for tomorrow."

"Really? What happened? Was it an intentional attack?"

"Most electronic attacks are, so yes, but not like you're thinking. A certain reporter, who shall remain nameless for the time being, was visiting sites he shouldn't have. Or not during work time and on work machines anyway."

"Ah."

"Yeah. So, what about you? How's the case going?"

"Also frustrating. It's gonna be a complicated one, I think."

"Dangerous enough to warrant the temporary will?" The quiet concern in her voice causes me to pause, and she sighs. "Your silence speaks volumes."

I shake my head, despite knowing she can't see it. "No, no, I was just considering the answer. It's really not as straightforward as that. We have footage of the culprit, but no idea who they are or what they're after, so in terms of danger, I honestly don't know yet. I mean, I'm armed, and Bert's here as well, which is usually enough to reduce pretty much any danger, eh?"

Lori laughs. "It's funny, but your tone? It sounds like you're more worried about me being worried than you are about the person you're after. Even after writing a will."

I smile. "I am. I don't want you worrying too much."

"Though with your job, it's something I've kinda gotta get used to, right? Anyway, if you have footage, you should be able to do a face match, at least."

"Unfortunately not. See, they're infecting cameras with some sort of virus. It means their face gets auto-censored on video. That was part of why I was calling. I was hoping maybe there'd been something similar in the press. I could use any tip-offs as a leaping-off point."

"And there was me thinking you just wanted to hear my voice."

There was a time I would have panicked at her statement, but I can hear the smile in Lori's voice, so I know she's only playing. "That too. But the faster I solve the case, the faster I can get to spending time with you, eh."

"Nice try. I'll have you know using your girlfriend as a source is rather cheeky. I'd charge you if I thought I was going to be of much use."

"Ah, so there's nothing going around?"

"Nothing to do with censorship, no. Or nothing I've heard anyway. We tend to keep each other up to date in New Hopeland, so I would have thought we'd have been informed if one of the other news providers had heard anything. Of course, with the computers down, I can't run a check for you yet. Once we're back up, I'll see what I can find before I leave."

"That would be great, thank you."

"Oh, you'll definitely thank me, even if I find nothing."

A blush rises to my cheeks and I get to my feet, because you can totally walk embarrassment off, right? I cross the room and slide the balcony doors open. "You're making me blush in front of a client," I say, once I'm in the safety of the outside.

"Yup. I'm terrible, me." Lori laughs. "Seriously, though, if you'd rather I didn't, that's fine. I can always tease you later."

"I would love to play more, but honestly, this is a tough one. I should probably concentrate on the case."

"That's fair enough. My second break is almost over anyway; you had some lucky timing there. So, I tell you what. I'll get back to work, and if I find anything, I'll send you what I can. We can pick *this* up another time. Not knowing how long this is all going to take, though, I better say good night now. So, good night, Cassie."

"Good night, Lori."

I hang up and smile to myself, letting the cool air wash over me. It's not a bad view up here, really. Sure, most of it is the adjacent building, but the lights in the distance behind are pretty, especially with the dark setting in early this time of the year. The street below is empty right now too. *Well, apart from...wait...*

I frown. There's only one person on the street, and he's walking along, completely oblivious to the world around him, his eyes dead set ahead. Even from up here, I recognize the way he walks and the slight tenseness in his shoulders. I can't see it, but his face will be serious. It'll be giving him a sense of natural power and authority, especially when paired with the Vancouver police department uniform he's wearing. I recognize it all because, though the angle I'm watching from is different, it's the *exact* walk I saw on the news all those years ago. It's the exact walk I used to see every day when he worked on a hard case.

"Dad?"

The question slips out in a near whisper as I watch the man below walk on. Without thinking, I bring my hand up and rub my eyes, trying to clear out any imaginary dirt that could be causing me to see something so impossible. When I look back again, the man is gone.

I must be getting tired, I tell myself and head back inside.

Dr. Faraday is still on the phone. Good. I clearly need a coffee. And a moment to compose myself.

So, I head to the kitchen and start the process of waking myself up. As if by magic, the near silence in the room is washed away by the *clack-clack* of a gargoyle checking on its master. "Caw," Bert says as he enters the room. He scrambles up the side of the worktop and marches along to stand closer to me, then reiterates, "Caw."

"Tired, Bert. Just tired." I rub his shiny head, and he settles into relaxed pose. "Thanks, though."

With my milk-free wake-up juice in hand, or rather in a mug in my hand, I beckon to Bert and say, "Come on."

We walk back into the room and I make my way back to the couch, where I sit quietly, sipping at my scalding hot drink until Dr. Faraday finishes with her calls. "Well, that was far less straightforward than I'd hoped," she says, joining me. Bert gets up and clambers over the back of the couch to make space for her to sit.

"Service providers. Nightmares to work with sometimes, but usually necessary for comfortable living. In a way, I feel a kinship with them."

Faraday smiles. "Yes, well, the necessity of *your* services is far less pleasant than the television, I'm sure."

"Depends what you're watching. Is it all getting sorted?"

"Yes. Though I am looking at around a week for someone to get out here to me."

"Then let's try to get everything resolved before then. I was speaking to a link I have with the press in case there's been anything similar floating around in terms of the censorship issue. Turns out there's nothing they can think of."

"I could have told you that would be a dead end. The press is a strange beast, Caz. It only reports what it's beneficial to report, and what is tailored to *its* audience. This sort of thing is more likely to turn up on the sites *I* visit than the mainstream."

I roll my eyes. "Without solid proof, you're absolutely right. But not everyone is as cynical as you are. Many would still try to sell the story, and the mainstream pays more. On top of that, most of them keep their ears to the ground in case there's something interesting to keep an eye on even if it seems a little out there initially."

She snorts a short laugh. "Well, I shall leave you to your faith then. Who knows? Perhaps you are correct, and they will now go looking."

I raise an eyebrow Faraday's way. "Sounds like someone doesn't care much for the press in general. You haven't had any run-ins with reporters, have you?"

"Oh, God no. I just resent their lack of giving page time to some of the more important stories. Or what I would deem important anyway. Is that selfish of me?"

"I don't think selfish is the right word, no. But you do clearly hold your own views very highly above those of the masses. If you're considering whether that breaks the illusion, I wouldn't worry about it. Self-indulgence is common, in a variety of forms. It's a shame, though. A lead would be nice at this point. Are you certain Jonah is the only one where you work who knows what you are?"

"As certain as I can be. He's the only one who has been mentioned to me."

"Could he have some others set up to watch covertly?"

"If he does, they aren't mentioned in my files." She catches my expressions and confirms, "I like to snoop."

"I see. How many people have access to your files?"

"HR can see my general files. The ones showing what I am, though? Only Mr. Burrell."

"And you."

She shakes her head. "No, I go in in using *his* details. He is the only one with legitimate access. I suppose someone else *could* do the same, but why would they be looking at my files?"

I shrug. "Someone could have their suspicions something's up. Maybe you slipped up and didn't realize it? Or they could have gone looking for something else and started searching *all* the private files. I'm sure there are plenty of those, eh?"

"There are, though I only look at my own when I go in there."

"This is all working on the idea someone knows or suspects *something,* though. We should really look at some other possibilities. Have you rejected anyone recently?"

"Rejected?"

"Yeah. Like, did anyone ask you out for a drink or anything?"

"Ah, on a date, you mean. No, nothing like that. Honestly, most of the people I meet are either already with someone or they aren't interested in me in that way. I think I *intrigue* some of my fellow staff, but most of them are a little scared of me. Or that's the way it seems, anyway. But I *am* the boss of many of them in terms of position. Still...there were a few meeting requests I declined."

"Meeting requests?"

"Yes. A few people in the forums and discussion groups expressed a desire to meet up IRL. Or 'in real life' if you prefer. I declined."

"Any particular reason?"

"Because I'm not an idiot. I don't truly know who most of these people are, and our one shared interest is not enough for me to risk exposing myself. My social life is a mix of a small number of work colleagues and a few conspiracy hunters from local groups. I feel more comfortable having the minor level of control that comes with knowing they are from around here. And no, I don't expect any of them to be responsible for this either."

"Okay, so let's talk about the ones you…"

I hear a low growl from somewhere behind me, cutting my words off, and turn my head to see Bert staring intently at the door. "Keep talking," I say, slowly rising to my feet.

I'm not sure what Dr. Faraday is saying, as I'm concentrating on remaining quiet. I creep across the room and tap the button under the decorative painting by the door. The image flickers and is replaced by a shot of the hallway outside. The screen is taken up almost entirely by the face of the doctor's stalker. Of course, it's already censored. "Bert, stay. Guard Dr. Faraday."

"Caw."

"Shut the door after me and don't open it until I get back," I tell Dr. Faraday.

"Of course," Faraday replies.

I pull my gun out from the holster and reach for the door release button. Obviously sensing what's going on, the person on the screen turns and takes off. "*Diu,*" I growl, and grab the now unlocked door, throwing it open as I dash through.

"Stop," I yell, but I already know the runner won't. They round the corner at the end of the hallway, and I force myself to speed up. I hit the corner and turn just in time to see the doors to the elevator at the far end pull shut. The light starts descending. The second elevator is already here, so I jump in and hit the button for the ground floor, guessing that's where the first is heading. I reach my destination quickly and run out. The other elevator is also there, the doors shut.

"Has anyone come out?" I yell to the security desk.

"What? Oh, what the..." the guard says, having obviously seen my gun. Good job I was introduced to this one. "No, it came down and just stopped."

"Did you notice it stop on any floors after the fifth?"

"I don't think so. I can check, though."

"You do that," I say and hit the door-open button. I step back and raise my Glock, pointing it squarely at...an empty elevator.

"The log indicates no stops," the guard says.

I nod and step inside. No sign of anyone tampering with the roof panels. "Does this thing have a security camera?"

"Of course. You want me to check it?"

"Yeah."

"Okay, hold on...well, that's weird."

"What's wrong?"

"The camera has been turned. It's not facing into the elevator anymore."

I frown and walk over to the security desk. The guard lets me see without question. "Can you access the cameras on the fifth floor?"

"Sure." He clicks a button, and we start viewing a selection of shots from cameras now facing walls. "Well, shit."

"AND THAT'S ABOUT all of it." I sigh. "Security footage showed whoever it was entered the hall and turned the cameras shortly before we got back. Given what happened, it means they knew I'd give chase too."

Dr. Faraday rubs her chin thoughtfully. "You're right, it does seem clear they knew you'd try following them. But why didn't they come back here after you went down to the ground?"

"At first, I thought Bert may have been a deterrent but..." I shake my head. "If that were the case, I doubt they would have come here at all, just in case I set him on them. No. I don't think this was about you. Or not tonight, anyway. They know who I am, and they know why I'm here. This feels like they were challenging me."

"Why would they do that?"

"I don't know. Either they have a personal reason to target me, or they're trying to tell me I'm powerless to stop them. Either way, it just makes me more determined to catch them." I relax back into the couch a little and ask, "I don't suppose you can think of any new residents? Maybe one who appeared just before or after the problems started? Security weren't aware of any."

"None I know of. Though I suppose making themselves known to me would make them too obvious a potential suspect."

"Or just a friendly person."

"True. While you were gone, I put something together, by the way. It should be accessible through the Case Tool."

I glance toward the Doc. "What is it?"

"All the details I could gather on the people who I rejected for IRL meet-ups. Usernames, known contact details, where I spoke to them, when, and a general idea of the content of our conversations."

"You work fast."

"More so when I'm panicked."

"And when you have a tight deadline, I bet."

"That, Caz, is when I'm panicked the most."

Chapter Four

THE LIGHT STARTS to creep through the darkness, bringing with it a heaviness on my chest. I blink and, when that fails to clear the cobwebs, raise a hand to rub my eyes. The first thing that comes into view is a sharp, metal beak. "What the..."

I sit up, and Bert tumbles off my chest and onto my knees with a clunk. I stifle a yelp but pull my legs up and hug them through the bedsheet anyway. Bert scrambles to his feet and protests. "Caw."

"Hey, don't you take that tone with me. Since when do you rest on my chest? And when did I move over here?"

"That, I am afraid, is my fault. On both counts." Dr. Faraday enters through the kitchen door, carrying with her a mug of steaming something. From the rich aroma in the air, it's a new coffee. She holds it out to me, and I take it while she clarifies. "You fell asleep at the computer. I didn't think it would be too comfortable, so I carried you to the couch. It was cold, too, so I thought the cover would be appreciated."

"And Bert?"

"Once I covered you, he clambered on and refused to get off until I backed away. Even then he was cuddled up under one of your arms, ready to climb back on whenever I even so much as glanced over at you. It was sweet really, seeing him move slowly to avoid disturbing you, but keeping a glare on me."

"Ah, he was being protective." I give my little beast a rub on the head and say, "Good Bert."

"Caw," he replies, then waddles off, chest slightly pushed out.

"In fairness to him, I'd have rather you didn't carry me. I appreciate the thought, but I'd have preferred you to just wake me."

"Yes, well, I thought if I did that, you'd try to continue working. Given the events of last night, rest seemed like it would do you better than overdoing it."

"I'm that transparent, eh? I *had* finished, though, or I wouldn't have let myself drift off. You'd be surprised how easily I can sleep in different places too. At least when it's needed."

Faraday smiles. "I didn't peg you for being that adaptive, at least not outside a working capacity."

"That's good. Plenty of human-like ability to offend there. Good job I'm so thick skinned. If you must know though, I *am* a creature of habit. When I'm not working, there are only two places I can sleep comfortably right now, maybe three if you include my couch. Everywhere else is equally as uncomfortable, but a necessity for work. Since this is a job, I deal with it."

"In other words, you're stubborn."

"In the face of discomfort, yes. Anyway, if it happens again, nudge me. I'll be more comfortable with it, and Bert won't start viewing you as overstepping the boundaries."

"Noted. How is he with your partner out of interest? If that's too personal, you don't have to answer. I'm just curious."

I take a mouthful of coffee and think about it. There doesn't seem to be any harm in answering. She may even be able to help me a little. "Good coffee," I comment, then continue, "He's fine with her. She's a Tech Shifter, though, and we haven't introduced him to her shifted side. With your professional face on, do you think he'd have an issue with her like that?"

"Good question." Faraday wrinkles her nose a little, crosses her arms, and looks up at the ceiling. "Honestly, I'm not sure. If he's fine with her normally, he'd likely recognize her and continue to view her just the same in her gear. That's assuming there isn't a reason for him to be on high alert, of course. Like today, there was certainly reason for him to be more protective even though he generally seems to view me as not being a threat. Honestly, there's no way to be certain other than for you to test it. But I would recommend doing so during a peaceful period. And slowly. If it helps any, I can go through his most recent log output while I'm in the office today just to check what sort of labels and indicators he has assigned to her. You said her name was Lori, correct?"

"That's right. And thank you, that would be a big help."

"Okay, I'll check it out. And now we both better get ready. My shift starts in an hour and a half."

I nod. "No problem. Oh, what did you do with the file I was working on, by the way? I'm going to need it today."

"I thought you might. I saved it and put it through the Case Tool."

"Good," I say, and head toward the bathroom.

"STILL NO HANSON?" I ask.

"No," Devereaux replies, sitting back into his chair and crossing his arms behind his head. He sways idly from side to side as he adds, "Honestly, I'm getting quite worried. Her sleep pattern has been *really* messed up."

"So, what? Is she sick?"

"She is now, but that wasn't what caused it. You've known her longer than me. Has she ever mentioned anything...I don't know, traumatic, or anything like that?"

I smile. "Not for her. Why's that?"

"She's not sleeping because she's been hallucinating."

I frown and lean forward. "Hallucinating what?"

"I don't know. I've asked, but all she says is bad memories."

I stare off at the wall. *Bad memories, eh? Sounds like we're both having the same trouble.*

"You okay?"

The concern in Deveraux's voice draws me back, and I nod. "Yeah. Sorry. I had a similar thing, that's all."

"Really? When? What happened?"

I shake my head. "Nothing to see here, I'm afraid. Or nothing that would help Hanson. I thought I saw my dad walking along outside my client's place last night, that's all. It was getting dark and I was already tired, so I put it down to overwork and the timing."

"Fair enough."

I note the little hint of sadness in Devereaux's voice. He's worried and reaching for whatever he can find. I get that. I've seen plenty of clients go through the same thought process, Lori included back when she hired me to look into her brother's death. I can distract him at least, even if only for a short while. "So, what have we got on my three names?"

"Oh yeah, sorry," he replies, handing me a couple of sheets of paper. "So, the first one turned out to be a Terry Gavelle. He was arrested three months ago for armed robbery."

"It says here he was also charged with aggravated assault?"

"Yeah. I can't legally tell you more than that, because it's the only bit available to the public, but reading the file on screen, it's nasty stuff. He's being detained in a cell at his local station while he awaits trial and is currently causing a lot of trouble for the staff by the look of it. He probably still has computer access, albeit monitored, if he cited the correct human rights laws."

"He must have, because he was trying to arrange a meeting with my client."

"I wouldn't recommend it."

"She wasn't interested even without knowing all this, so no problems there. Okay, so the next one is…Tasha Clarke."

"Yup. Minor offence on record for shoplifting in her teens, but nothing since. I didn't tell you this, but she lives at the other end of the country, and her social media accounts make it clear she's on holiday abroad right now."

"Okay. So that just leaves door number three."

Devereaux nods. "Paul Raster. No criminal record at all, but we did run a check for him not so long ago."

I smile. This sounds promising. "He's local?"

"Yeah. Easily traceable too. His photo on the printout is taken from his employer's website. No idea what he does there, though."

"Okay, so who's the employer?"

"Shall I just pretend you snapped a shot of the photo and reverse image searched it yourself?"

"Saves me a job."

Devereaux laughs. "Okay, fine. I'll let you off because of the type of case you're working. He works at the main office for FE Limited."

I STICK MY cell phone onto speaker mode and dial Dr. Faraday. She answers after three rings just as I pull out into traffic.

"Caz. Have you found something?"

To the point. I like it. "Does the name Paul Raster mean anything to you?"

"It sounds...familiar. Should I know it?"

"He was the guy behind one of your real-life meet-up requests. He also works at Familiar Enterprises Limited's main office, the same as you."

Dr. Faraday goes silent for a moment, then replies, "Are you heading this way?"

"Of course."

"Okay. Give me a moment, and I'll check which section he's working in."

"You have access to the HR records?"

"Not really. Or I shouldn't, rather. It's easy enough to get in there with my level of access, though. There we go. Ah, yes, I do recognize him. He's a tour guide."

"A tour guide? That doesn't sound like someone who'd be able to home brew the tech we're looking at."

"No. From my limited interactions with him, it seems like...how can I put this? If we, as in the engineers, are experts, he's a hobbyist working on projects of a far simpler level. He understands the basics, albeit with no demonstrable ability to apply them, other than through verbal explanations."

"Which would essentially be enough to have most people on the tour being buried under the jargon."

"Quite."

"Unless he's hiding some skill."

"Also a possibility. How close are you?"

"A couple of blocks. Why?"

"Tour guides work half-day shifts. His ends in thirty minutes."

"That gives me plenty of time to find a suitable spot to watch him leave. I'll tail him home and see if he does anything unusual."

"Okay. If he loses you, I'll send you his address."

"Sure. But don't risk too much delving into the HR stuff. Unless it's necessary."

"Of course."

"Okay, well, I'll update you later. Keep safe."

I hang up and park just across the road from the offices and cut the engine. It starts quickly enough that I shouldn't have to worry. Plus, even if he leaves straight away, I'm going to be looking at a long wait which is not only a waste of power, but highly suspicious looking. So, I sit back and wait. And wait. And wait.

Eventually, my target *does* leave the building, stopping to chat with the security guard on the way. He gets into a small electric car near the front of the parking lot, and pulls up to the gate, giving me ample time to start my own engine. Once he's out, I start to follow, keeping a nice, legally regulated distance between my car and his. Just to keep my suspicion levels down, I even let a couple of cars pull in front of me. A small reduction in speed, albeit one that keeps me within the city minimum, and I have plenty of opportunity to check which way he turns.

And that's important. The films where someone says, "Hey, we're being followed"? It's always because they've seen the car heading the same way as them for a few blocks. And there's never another car in between them. Fiction it may be, but it rings true. At the very least if the person you're following has something to hide. People like that tend to be either careful or paranoid. I relate easier to the latter. Either way, Paul Raster is my only real suspect right now, so I have to work to the idea he *does* have something to hide.

As it happens, the address isn't too far from the FE Limited offices, so the journey doesn't take me much further than six or seven blocks. I park the car across the road from the house Paul Raster enters, and lean back into my seat, crossing my arms. Something doesn't feel right here.

"If this is where he lives, he's a little closer to work than Dr. Faraday. Walking it shouldn't be a big deal, so why drive? He's in the opposite direction to the apartment block too. Okay, think. Three options. One, he's keeping up appearances. His car is too crappy for it to be a status thing, so it would have to be to give a subtle hint it's not him. He's been in and gone and by a different means of transport than the stalker.

"Two, he has a need to get back. If it's not him, that could be anything. Online appointments or someone he cares for are the most likely. If it *is* him, though, it'd be to get ready. Change into the stalker suit, monitor anything he's been picking up, that sort of thing. Option three is he's just plain lazy."

I drum my fingers on the dashboard, keeping my eyes on the house for signs of movement. "Okay, let's see if he's getting any unusual incoming signals. That should at least either confirm or disprove the monitoring to a degree."

I grab the ping box from the glove compartment, place it on the dashboard, and tap the top. The holographic display lights up and I say, "Ping box. Initiate area scan, long range, target...eastwards. Cover area one hundred and twenty meters. Search for all active incoming and outgoing signals and confirm recipient registrations. Notify once complete."

The box beeps and the familiar line moves back and forth across the display.

"Okay, now I wait."

Beep.

I frown and look at the screen. The ping box has an outgoing signal hit already. The recipient is coming up as a mass of jumbled numbers and letters, meaning it's masked pretty tightly. Judging by the location, it's...in the car. *My car.* "Ping box, store details of hit and copy to server using standard file path."

My cell phone starts to ring, and my eyes drift over the display. Dr. Faraday. "It's a tracer," I mutter, and grab the phone. I hit answer and ask, "It's not Paul Raster, is it?"

"No."

"Okay, I'm on my way," I say, flicking the ping box to off and starting the engine. I throw both it and the phone onto the passenger side seat. "What's happening?"

"They're down behind the building. I can see them through the window."

"Do they know where *you* are?"

"They're looking directly at the window, so I'm guessing yes."

"Have you told security?"

"No. I...I still want to keep them out of this if I can."

I take a corner at speed and almost drift into oncoming traffic, but right myself quickly. That's the joy of these old police vehicles, they're built for this stuff. "I get what you're saying, but if things start looking bad, you may have to. Okay, look, I'm about three—no, two blocks away, and I'm keeping you on speaker until I get there. What are they doing now?"

"Hold on...they're looking at their phone."

"Right out the back of the building?"

"Yes."

"Is there any direct way in from that end?"

"None. You'll have to come through the front."

"Got ya. I'm pulling up now."

"Okay. They...they just put their phone in their pocket and..."

"What is it?"

"They just waved at me. They're walking away. Toward the back wall."

"I'm on it."

I leap out of the car and run into the FE Limited parking lot, drawing my Glock. Somewhere in the background someone is shouting. *Probably security. Just keep moving. I'm not letting them get away.*

I round the back of the building just in time to spot the stalker scaling the wall. It's big, but there are plenty of gaps to wedge your foot in. It's essentially a thick, solid fence.

"Hey!" I shout and bring my gun up. I squeeze the trigger, sending a bullet crashing against the metal. Before I can tell if I managed to shock them into stopping like I planned, a heavy weight slams into my back, knocking me face first to the floor.

"I've got her," the man on my back says.

"Not me, you idiot," I yell. "The person climbing the fence. Get them."

"Nice try," they say, and I crane my neck to look toward the wall. The stalker has leaped down over the other side and is moving at speed. And now they're gone.

"*Diu.*"

"*THAT* IS WHO I was going after," I growl, slamming my finger into one of the screens in the main security guard office. It hurts because I'm apparently too annoyed to control my vicious pointing skills, but the satisfying *clunk* of flesh meeting glass also leads to an even more satisfying flinch from Mr. Stops-Me-Ending-This-Case, so I'll ignore the pain.

The hapless guard frowns at the screen and asks, "What's up with the image distortion on their face?"

"It's some sort of software they've installed everywhere they're likely to be seen." He opens his mouth to say something and I cut him off. "No, I don't know what exactly it is, how it got on your systems, or how to remove it. I suggest getting your tech guys on it in case they come back. Maybe you'll get lucky and catch them before they can reinstall whatever it is."

He sighs. "Yeah, I guess you're right. I'm really sorry about that. But, I mean, you have to understand my position, right?"

I glare at him and he shrinks back a little. I read the news sites, so I know what he's worried about. "I'm not in the habit of collecting frequent sue-er miles."

"This was partially my fault, anyway." Dr. Faraday shifts uncomfortably in her seat and adds, "I didn't want people knowing."

"I get it. My sister went through some stuff a while back and didn't want to tell anyone either." The guard nods toward me. "Did you want me to list her as a daily guest in case she needs to rush around again? I can probably get her some mild clearance without having to say too much."

"That would be appreciated," Faraday replies.

"Check your footage and let me know if you find out how they got in too," I add. "The Doc'll give you my number."

"Yeah. No problem."

I get to my feet. "And so you know, I'm gonna be across the road checking something out, so don't start thinking I'm up to anything untoward, eh?"

I leave the room and start heading toward the main door. Dr. Faraday catches up before I make it across the main hall. "Caz, wait. I just wanted you to know I'm sorry. I didn't expect something like that to happen."

I shrug. "It was always a possibility. Look, as much as I'd love to tell you how cluing security in about me should have been your first point of call, what's done is done. It may not be a complete loss anyway."

"If we find something on the cameras you mean?"

I stop and shake my head. "No. They're too careful for that. All we're likely to get is to see them moving toward their watch spot. How are you with cars?"

"I know a little. I would recommend using a mechanic if there's an issue, though."

"Not exactly," I reply and start walking. "Come with me."

We cross to where my car is parked and I explain. "While I was watching Raster, I set my ping box to check for signals. I was hoping to trace something back to the ones in your apartment. It found something pretty quickly, but not in Raster's house."

Dr. Faraday narrows her eyes. "In your car?"

"Exactly. It wasn't precise as far as where in the car, but I know there shouldn't be any outgoing signals coming from it. At least not right then. Now, when you say you know a little, would you be likely to spot something out of place in a car?"

"Perhaps."

"Good. Because unless it's something I've seen before, I'm not going to have a clue."

I unlock the door and push my key into the ignition, then slide a panel aside to the right of the steering wheel. I tap a few buttons and the sound of metal scraping on metal rings out. The inbuilt jack poles slide down and pushes the car slightly off the floor. Not as high as an external jack would, but enough to fit under the car at least. The automatic illumination also helps.

Dr. Faraday slides under next to me and stares up at the clear layer covering the visible mechanical parts. "Reinforced glass?"

"Bullet and shatterproof, and in theory, safe against minor explosives."

"I thought it looked like an old squad car. This confirms it."

"It's not what you know, it's who you know," I comment, glancing over the parts for anything obvious.

Faraday slides down a little. "There's no sign of anything being forced. These panels are all fob locked, so it'd be clear if anyone had done anything to break in."

"They're fob locked?"

Faraday glances toward me, a bemused smile on her synthetic lips. "You didn't know?" I shake my head, and she taps one of the locks. "You can tell by the indent. There'll be a small fob on your keys. You just click it in, give a quarter turn to the left, and it unlocks the whole panel."

"The keys came with a fob, but I didn't know what it was for. It's in one of the drawers in my kitchen now."

"Didn't you ask whoever you got the car from?"

"And let them know I'm completely clueless? Not a chance."

"Hmm. Well, the main thing is, unless someone broke into your apartment with the intent of ransacking your kitchen, they wouldn't be able to get up in here."

The logical part of my brain says it can't be under here because to get to the fob, they'd have had to neutralize Bert at home first. My paranoia engine responds with *unless they did it* after *you started staying with Dr. Faraday.*

"Unlikely as it is," I say finally, "can you see anything?"

"Plenty. But nothing that would be emitting an unexpected signal."

We slide back out and I get the car back to its regular position on the floor. Next, I pop the trunk. Faraday looks in and says, "The bag, maybe?"

I see her reaching for it but snatch it away first, a blush rising to my cheeks. "That's my overnight bag for when I stay with Lori."

"Ah, your girlfriend. Say no more."

"I prefer partner. Girlfriend sounds so high school. Anyway, I'll check this." I kick myself mentally for how embarrassed my voice sounded and drop the bag into the back seat while Faraday buries herself in the other general junk.

While she rummages, I unzip the bag and start pulling things out. The jeans and T-shirt combo aren't too bad. Nor are the sleep shorts and cami top if I'm being honest. The lacier—not to mention skimpier—items are enough to make me die a little. I mean, I know Lori likes them. And yes, her reaction does make me feel sexy, which goes a long way to staving off my inner body critic, but...

You bought these together and don't want anyone else seeing them other than who they were intended to impress. You're not embarrassed, you're just protective of your relationship.

I smile and mumble, "Thanks, inner monologue. I'm using that one."

Thankfully, there's no sign of anything unexpected in the bag, so I don't have to worry about anyone other than Lori picturing me in awkward attempts to look confident. Well, and the store clerk. And anyone who saw me choosing...*No, shut up and work.*

"Nothing I can see," Faraday says. "You don't have many electronics here. A portable Familiar charger, and other assorted chargers, but nothing at all like I expected for a PI."

I walk around and throw the bag back in. I pull the trunk shut and walk around to the front of the car again. "I have a mixed relationship with technology."

I tap a few more keys, and the hood pops open. The engine parts are illuminated by the built-in lighting, much like the underside of the car. I stare into the mass of mechanics, and my eyes glaze over a little. "What am I looking at here?"

"Confirmation of something I suspected," Dr. Faraday says. "You see, a lot of these parts are slightly older than most modern vehicles use. Some of them look like...yes, like the gas pump here. It's a disused model."

"So, what are you saying?"

"Law enforcement likely has contracts with manufacturers to ensure they get to keep the more robust systems even when the public can't any longer. Sometimes, the best form of progress is to stand still, after all."

"I haven't heard that one before. I'll remember it next time someone questions the tech I *do* use."

Faraday leans over and peers down between the parts. She squints a little, reaches in, and pulls out a small disc about six millimeters thick. "It was between the lower part of the engine and the lighting."

"How did you spot that?" I ask, turning the small chunk of metal over in my hand.

"There was a strangely circular shaped black spot on the pipe, meaning something had to be casting a shadow. Given the lighting is supposed to help find faults and damage, it seemed rather strange. To be fair, if I hadn't been looking for something subtle, I wouldn't have noticed it."

I nod and retrieve the ping box from the front passenger seat. I place it down, tap the top, and wait for the holographic display. I place the metal disc on top and say, "Ping box. Initiate item scan. Cross-reference with stored details and confirm if match found. Notify once complete."

We wait for a few seconds, then hear a *beep*.

I pick up the disc and read over the display. "It matches the signal I picked up earlier. My guess is it's a tracer."

"It doesn't look branded. I know commercial tech is legally supposed to be. Could it be home brew?"

"Oh, it *is* branded," I say, smiling proudly that I finally appear to know something my client doesn't. It's childish, sure, but since she knows the inner workings of my car better than me, I figure it's fair play. I push the hood closed and show her the side of the disk. "You see these ridges? That's the branding. Let's see...the red line right there is the start of it. Hang on."

I grab my phone and open a scanning app, then align the red line on the side with the one on the screen. When prompted by the screen, I start to slowly rotate the disk until the red line has completed a full circle and is back in line with the screen mark. After a few seconds, the app loads up a diagram of the scan and asks if I want to proceed. I tap yes and explain, "Security companies who work with smaller items have this system. It's kinda like a bar code of sorts. You see them on some gun parts too. And here we go. The app says the code marks it as a tracer sold by a local merchant named Joe Farrah."

There's a pause, then Dr. Faraday asks, "You know him, don't you?"

I become aware of the dark look that's fallen across my face. I banish it with a slightly annoyed smile. "Yeah, I do. You better get back to work. I'll check this out."

I GIVE THE door to the shop a good, hard push, sending it clanging against the wall behind it. Clearly used to such behavior from potential customers, the current shop assistant just smiles and asks, "How can we help you this fine day?"

"You can help by getting me Joe Farrah."

"Mr. Farrah is..."

"Is somewhere in here," I cut in. "He's not the sort to leave the shop entirely to someone else, eh?"

"I was going to say the boss is upstairs."

I cross my arms and lean against the nearest wall. "Okay, good. Can you go and get him?"

The young man waits a moment and then gives me a patronizing wave, beckoning me to continue.

I sigh and say, "Please?" Sure, it was through gritted teeth, but it was still sort of polite.

Satisfied, the young man nods and asks, "Who shall I say wants to speak to him?"

I smile. "O'Brien."

He steps behind the counter and opens a door but doesn't fully leave the room. Instead, he leans through into the next room and yells, "Boss! There's someone called O'Brien here to see you."

"O'Brien? For fuck's sake. Hang on." A clattering sound rings out from somewhere above us, and the angry footfalls of someone who's about to get even angrier come down the stairs. Joe Farrah steps into the room, grumbling. "This better be important...Cassie Tam?"

The sales assistant frowns. "Tam? I thought you said your name was O'Brien?"

"No, you asked me who you should say was calling. I never said O'Brien was *my* name." I turn off the innocent smile I've been flashing and give Joe a serious look. "We need to talk."

"Like hell we do." He turns to walk away.

"Hey," I say and throw the tracer toward him. "Catch."

Joe snatches the small disk out of the air without looking. If he weren't a member of the King's Guard, the elite group who know the truth about who rules the New Hopeland Underworld, I'd be surprised. He turns it over in his hand and says, "A tracker."

"Obviously. I have a few questions about it."

"Not interested," he says and walks back through the door.

"Well, I am," I reply and jump less than gracefully over the counter to follow. To his credit, the assistant knows better than to try to stop me.

"I could have you arrested, you know," Joe growls, continuing his walk back up the stairs.

"Yeah, well, so could a lot of people." I follow him and state, "That was in my car. Hidden in the engine. I found it with the ping box you sold my partner, so thanks for that. It works great, by the way. Good price she got too. What was it she mentioned? A photo from Kansas? Care to enlighten me as to what that's about?"

"Great," he replies, ignoring my questioning. "So, someone wanted to know where you were. Deal with it, detective, I have my own problems."

"I bet you do. Keeping hold of store staff must be one of them with your attitude."

He stops in place and slowly turns his head to give me a dark look over his shoulder. "Attitude problems? Coming from you, that's real cute. You know nothing about who I am, or who I was. Some of us can't outrun our ghosts forever. So, kindly fuck off."

I notice the bags under his eyes. *I guess Hanson isn't the only one having trouble sleeping.*

I sigh. "Fine. You know what, Joe? You don't like me, I get it. But this isn't about me. The person who put it in my car is stalking my client. They're getting by the security at her workplace, following her home, and seemingly disappearing into thin air. I need to know who bought that thing, so I can put a stop to what they're doing."

"A stalker, huh? You got a warrant?"

"For you? No. Doesn't mean I can't get one."

"Yeah. I figured as much." He grunts, turns around, and walks back down the stairs, shoving past me as he goes. I follow him into the back room, and he slumps into a cheap computer chair. He taps the switch on the monitor on the desk in front of him. His fingers fly over the keyboard, and he comments, "I knew you were trouble the moment you got brought up, you know that?"

"Gotta love a good reputation. The LV case wasn't exactly fun for me either."

"Yeah, well it just proved I was right about you. Not that the others ever believed me."

Well, that's gotten my attention. "You make it sound like the King's Guard have been talking about me for a while."

Joe ignores me and sits back into his chair, crossing his arms behind his permanently scowling head. He nods at the tracker disk on the desk. "According to my records, this should still be on the shelves. And it's new stock from two weeks...hang on. Hey! Sammy! Where's shelf A-thirty-two?"

There's a brief silence, then the assistant replies from the other room. "By the counter, fourth up. And my name's still John."

"All the while I'm paying you, your name is whatever I say it is." Joe makes a couple of clicks with the mouse, leans in to get a closer look at the screen, and then slams his fist on the table. "They fucking robbed me. That masked freak fucking robbed me."

Masked freak? I step toward Joe. "Say that again."

Chapter Five

ON THE SCREEN, the now familiar censored stalker stands outside Joe's shop. Initially, they just stare at the security camera, then turn their head and start looking away from the store. Eventually, they turn back to watch the camera again, before leaving. The video clip lasts a little under thirty seconds.

"This was the first time they came here?"

"That's right."

"And how long ago was this?"

Joe taps the time stamp on the screen and confirms, "About two and a half weeks. Though it weren't the first time I noticed them. That was this one."

He loads up a new clip, this time of the stalker opening the front door and walking straight into the store. They start looking over the shelves, running their hands over various items, and then freeze at the sound of Joe stating, "Stay right where you are."

The rise and fall in the stalker's shoulders gives away that they're laughing, albeit apparently silently. Slowly, they turn to face Joe, their face censored on the video. Joe steps forward on screen, holding what appears to be a shotgun.

"Really? A shotgun? A bit overkill, don'tcha think?"

"I got a right to defend my store, detective."

The video continues with the stalker slowly lowering their hands. Something flies out of one of their sleeves, and the room starts to fill with smoke. The sound of gunfire rings out, and Joe stops the video. "I missed."

"Which means they're quick, eh?"

"That and I can't aim for shit if I can't see." He rolls the video back a little and zooms in on the stalker's hands, just as he enters with the shotgun. As he moves the video slowly, it becomes clear the stalker did indeed grab one of the trackers from the shelves. "And there's where they got your tracker from. This clip's only a few days old."

I sigh. "So, let me guess. After this little meeting, you started going back through the security footage and found that first clip you showed me."

"And a bunch of others. They hung around outside the store every night for a couple of days."

"Okay. You called them a masked freak. When you confronted them, what did they look like?"

"Like a masked freak."

"I need more than that. Look, let's cut a deal. You tell me what the mask looked like and maybe let me have the two clips you showed me, and I'll tell you what I know about why the videos are censored."

He crosses his arms and glares at me. "Fine, but only 'cause I'm curious. It was dark, and the lights were off, so I couldn't see too much. It was clear they were wearing a mask, though. It looked pretty skintight, and the shape was human, but there was a shine to the fabric that gave it away. The lights from outside caught it, and it looked kinda rubbery. The face weren't one I recognized, though."

"That's it?"

"That's it. Now. Your turn."

"They've installed something on multiple cameras across the city. I'm not certain how it works, or how to get rid of it, but the most likely scenario is it picks up on something on the mask and automatically edits the videos. As far as I know, the edits can't be undone or removed."

"Great. And how did they get whatever software they're using onto my system?"

I shrug. "Damned if I know. That first clip you showed me? It probably happened shortly after that."

"What makes you say that?"

"They spent too long looking at the camera. They were either noting something about it or committing the location to memory. That's my guess."

Joe grunts. "I'm gonna have to strip and upgrade the whole security system. Again."

"You aren't the only one. Mind if I keep the tracker for now? Maybe I can trace it back to the source."

"Go ahead. It masks itself anyway, and it's not lightweight encryption. But you're welcome to try. Or give it to someone who knows what they're doing. Just bring it back afterwards. I can still sell it if you don't wreck it."

I SIT IN the driver's seat of my car and turn the tracker disk over in my hand a few times. "I could put it back in the engine. Chances are they're monitoring it and already know I've taken it back to Joe. They aren't dumb enough to think I literally drove the car into the store, so there's no element of surprise here."

I close my eyes and start running through what I know. "The body language, the brazen way they just go where they want, and the forward planning. They're arrogant. Or confident. Which means they probably won't stop monitoring the signal unless I destroy the thing. So,

I still have a chance to use it to my advantage. No sense in trying to fool them about me knowing, though.”

I throw the tracker into my glove compartment and start the engine. *I'll head back to the Doc's place for now and go through the two videos from Joe again. Maybe I'll be able to spot something on the big screen. Wait...*

I hit the brakes, skidding the car to a stop, and leap out through the door. Just up ahead, running down the alley in front of me, is the stalker. I give chase.

They were waiting for me. They aren't running as quickly as last time I chased them either. They want *me to know which way they're going.*

I draw my Glock and keep following. *Concentrate, Cassie. Don't let yourself get caught out like you did with the LV.*

I speed up, barely keeping my balance as I take the corner, and run right past someone. Someone familiar. Someone who causes me to stop in my tracks and turn around. I look the man up and down, and my arms drop to my side, the Glock clattering against the floor. “Dad?”

My father looks directly at me and speaks, his voice firm and resolute. “I blame you.” And just like that, he fades into smoke and disappears.

My legs start to wobble, and I drop to my knees, struggling to fight back the tears. I throw my head back and yell, “It wasn't my fault,” then slam my fist into the floor. “It wasn't my fault. You said you didn't blame me. You said...”

An image clicks in my mind. An old news interview. They'd asked Dad about the escalating crime in the local area. I can hear his response, loud and clear. “The people who see crimes and don't report it. The ones who commit crimes and don't care who they hurt. The people that stop *us* from doing our jobs. *I blame you.*”

The way he said those last three words. The clothes he wore. The way he stood. That was exactly what I just saw. Exactly.

I look over to where my father had stood moments ago, then grab my gun, holster it, and take my phone out of my pocket. It takes a moment to load, but I start up the video of the first time the stalker visited Joe's shop and pause it when they turn away from the camera. They're looking at something on the floor. Zooming in, I can just about make out the shape of the city's experimental environmental cleansing tool, an EU25 unit. Like the one in front of me.

I'm certain there was one outside the Doc's apartment block too. Joe hasn't been sleeping. If I'm right about this, then Faraday wasn't the original target. And that would mean I know who this is and part of what they're doing, just not why they're after the Doc. But how am I going to test this?

I take a deep breath and try to calm myself. The answer hits me. "Hanson."

I REACH HANSON'S apartment block in good time. Unlike mine, it has an underground parking lot with enough spaces for every apartment, plus one visitor for half of them again. It goes down a few stories. Four in fact. "The further down you go, the more stuff you can get buried under if something goes wrong," I grumble, my second lap of the top story proving conclusively there are no spaces on this tier. "*Diu.*"

Thankfully, I find somewhere on the second story down and manage to park pretty quickly. The whole thing is too big for me to call my unease claustrophobia.

Someone told me once the fear of being trapped is called cleithrophobia. That's more what this is, in a way. For the most part, I put it down to my ever-present paranoia.

I ignore the elevator up to the main building, choosing instead to take the stairs—quickly—back up and into the street. A swift walk around the building reveals what I expected. There are a few EU25s around the front of the building and the side Hanson's apartment is on. Satisfied I'm on the right track, I walk inside and make my way up to Hanson's floor. I can't remember her door number, but it's easy to find her place. She painted the door red once, entirely because she wanted to rebel against the building's strict rules on not using bright colors. It's not like she felt like they were unfair or anything, she was just bored. When that led to her being threatened with being booted out, she put it back to normal. She also meticulously studied the official guidelines for the building and found there was no rule explicitly stating she couldn't change the door handle. So, while hers *does* match the standard indented hand grip of every other door in the building, hers is not a muted silver, but rather features a red outer ring, with sharp jagged teeth painted on the black central bar. It's all kinds of cute and creepy.

I press the comms button next to the door and wait for the green light to signify I can speak. "Hanson, it's Cassie. Look, I know you're not feeling great, but this is important. Can you open the door?"

There's a pause, then Hanson's voice comes through. "Yeah. Yeah. Hold on."

After a few seconds, the door clicks and opens. Hanson has already turned away before she waves me in. "There's coffee in the pot," she says and makes her way over to a small armchair.

The apartment is mostly open plan, a bit like mine, but the furniture is more modern. I make my way over to the kitchen side and pour myself a mug of wake-up juice. "This smells strong. Aren't you supposed to be trying to sleep?"

"Can't. That'd be rude while I have a visitor."

I smile and nod at the pot. "Most of it's gone, Hanson. You're trying to *not* sleep."

She chuckles and builds into a laugh. "If only it were that easy."

I lean against the counter and sigh. "I know you've been hallucinating."

Hanson rolls her eyes. "Dev. I'll get him for that one."

"Look. You're not the only one."

She tilts her head and fixes her eyes on me. "Explain."

"Twice now, I've seen him. My dad, I mean. It was the anniversary of his death a few days ago, did you know that?"

"No. I'm sorry."

I shake my head. "It's fine. The first time, I wasn't sure it was him. The case I'm working? I've been staying with my client. I was on her balcony and I thought I saw him down on the street below." I notice Hanson wince. That means I'm heading the right way with this. "The second time, though, I know it was him."

"How?"

"It was earlier today. He was right there in front of me, so close I could have reached out and touched him if I wasn't so shocked." I smile and look down. "I half expected him to call me his little firecracker. He used to do that when I was working a frustrating case, because I could sometimes get a little angry and lash out."

"Surely not."

I smile. "This one's *really* frustrating. He didn't say it, which was odd. Do you know what he did say, though? He told me it was my fault."

Hanson frowns. "Didn't you say he told you…"

"He didn't blame me. Yeah. So, that's me. What about you? You been reliving some bad memories?"

"Bad cases. We all have at least one we wish went differently, right?"

I nod. "I need to know. When you've seen things, has it ever been in here?"

"Not at first. Now, it's every time I go to sleep. Hence my staying awake as much as possible. When it started, it was all…I'd catch things through the window. One time, I went running out into the hall, and I could still see…stuff…going on outside. By the time I got down there, they were all gone."

"Did you ever see anything while there were other people around? Where the hallucinations were?"

Hanson closes her eyes and clicks her tongue. "I don't think so. I don't know. Believe it or not, I'm not in the best way right now."

"It's fine. This helps." I take a big gulp of coffee. I could ask about the face censoring, but if she'd noticed anything, she would have mentioned it the last time we spoke. This is enough to help me.

Hanson yawns. "I'm not stupid, Cassie. You think you're onto something. You definitely didn't come just to catch up and do some joint venting."

"No, I didn't. I came for the coffee." I make sure Hanson is looking right at me and give her a subtle nod.

She returns it and replies, "It's good to talk. Maybe I'll try some more sleeping."

"I'll leave you to it. Stay safe, Hanson."

"You too. I'll let you let yourself out."

ONCE I'M OUTSIDE, I make my way down to my car and pull the ping box out of my pocket. I check the results. Nothing in Hanson's apartment is transmitting through anything other than Government and PD gateways. I cross my arms and focus.

What did Joe say? "You know nothing about who I am, or who I was. Some of us can't outrun our ghosts forever." It sounds like he's got the same problem. Whether I'm right about who this is or not, they're probably monitoring us, which means I can't confirm that yet. If Hanson was included on the list of fake King's Guard members during the LV case, it would all but prove I'm right.

So, how do I test it, just in case they don't take my bait? I need to speak to someone away from cameras that are transmitting. Who would know who was on the list?

I groan, pick up my phone, and hit dial on the number for the New Hopeland Prison.

"NHP."

"Hi, I was hoping to arrange a visit with one of the prisoners. A Malcolm Castleford..."

"Castleford?"

"Yeah. He was an accountant, got arrested for arranging a dog fight. Do you think it would be possible?"

"Hold on." The line goes silent for a moment, then the voice comes back. "Okay, sorry. I needed to check what I could say. The police are here now, though, and the press, so it's going to get out anyway. Malcolm Castleford is dead."

"Dead? What happened?"

"One of the other prisoners killed him..."

The phone clatters a little and another voice comes on. "Who is this?"

I sigh. "Cassie Tam, PI. I assume he wasn't meant to tell me that bit?"

"No, he was not. Until the press release, it needs to remain confidential. If you're a PI, you know how that works, don't you?"

"Of course. I'll keep it quiet."

"Good." They hang up.

I start the car and make my way out of the parking lot.

I have some time before I pick Faraday up from work. But who can I talk to? If I'm right about everything being monitored, I can't go to the police station to speak with Donal O'Brien. Devin Carmichael is an option, but meeting with him right now might make the stalker suspicious. The same applies to Fuerza, not that I want to make a habit of working with him anyway. If messages are being monitored, I'd need a new burner phone before contacting anyone anyway and even then, I don't know if they have a way to monitor that too. No, I'll work to the assumption I'm right and not get anyone else involved unless as a last resort. If they take the bait, I'll know anyway.

"YOU'VE BEEN QUIET," Dr. Faraday says as we enter her apartment.

"Like I said, I needed to think."

Bert clatters up to check on who entered, but from the casual speed he's walking, I'd guess he was pretty sure it was us. "Caw," he says, nodding our way.

"Hello, Bert," Faraday replies. "I hope you've been behaving yourself."

He lets out a mechanical clicking as he makes his upper and lower beak rapidly clatter together, then saunters off to sit on the couch.

"I can't see any damage," Faraday states, then walks toward the kitchen. "Did it help? The thinking?"

"To a point." I follow her in and rest myself against the door frame, arms crossed, while she starts making me a coffee. "There are a few loose ends I need to tie up, but I'm making progress."

"Well, that's certainly heartening to hear. I assume the visit to your friend Joe Farrah was fruitful?"

"We're not friends. He's made that plenty clear, and I'm not inclined to try to change his mind."

She laughs. "Your buttons are easy to push."

"Thanks," I grunt.

"Don't take it too seriously. That I'm in the mood to joke is a good thing. I've not really been in the right frame of mind of late."

"You seem to have been *pushing my buttons* easy enough," I reply, throwing a smile to show I'm not angry about it.

"Yes. I think you bring that out of people quite naturally. It's something to do with your reactions. You either give exactly the backlash you'd expect, or you just play right back. It's endearing, really. I expect Lori rather enjoys it."

"She does. Makes sense to me, though. If I'm being honest, I'm still struggling to get my head around you having moods. Or ones that are affected by things, anyway."

She pours me a coffee and replies, "That is because you like to look at things as very black and white. Good and bad, right and wrong, person and machine. Or that's the impression I get, anyway."

We make our way to the main room and I give Bert a light pat to get him to move up so I can sit down. "Sometimes, black and white is the best way to look at things."

"Undoubtedly. I rather suspect it makes your job easier. If you can distinguish the right and wrong outcome so clearly, it gives you a target to aim at. Some things are not so simple, though."

"They can be *made* simple. Take your not being the mood to joke around. That was a fear response, eh?" She nods, and I continue, "If we complicate it, it means facing my own uncertainty about whether what you feel constitutes a real emotion. If we boil it down to its base, it doesn't matter whether what you're feeling is real or not. It doesn't even matter if the response is real or simulated. It *does* affect you, and that's all there is to it. As my client, I take that into consideration."

"Yes, well, sometimes I wish it didn't. Mr. Burrell did a really good job with my fear responses. It's part of why I'm so interested in the things I am; a constant fear about what others are planning, especially those in power."

"Paranoia. We're well acquainted."

She smiles. "So. Now you're a little more relaxed, did you get anything useful from your meeting with Joe Farrah?"

I blink. "Great. A machine reads people better than I do." I sit back into the chair and take a big mouthful of coffee. "He's met your stalker before."

"Does he know who it is?"

I shake my head. "No. They were masked, and it was dark. They also stole the tracker we found in my car."

"Ah. And did you return it to him?"

"Only long enough for him to verify it. I put it back in the car, just not where we found it."

"So, they don't know you found it?"

"No, I'm pretty sure they know we found it, and that I know where it came from. I'm still hoping to trace it back to wherever it's transmitting to *if* I can't resolve this by other means."

"Why not run a trace on it anyway?"

"Because it masks itself. The chances are they'll have systems in place that will make it useless as a process too. My hope is their knowing what I've been looking into will spook them into making a move again. And this time, I won't let them get away."

Dr. Faraday sighs, and for a moment, I think I catch a mechanical *whirr* behind it. "I hope you're right. I just want this all to be over so I can get back to normalcy. What about you, Caz? What will you do after you catch them?"

"The same thing I always do. P and M.O.T.T.N.C."

"P and M.O.T.T.N.C?"

"Paperwork and Move On To The Next Case."

"Your normalcy is even more repetitive than mine. What about the money? You're not cheap." She catches my raised eyebrow and clarifies. "I'm not complaining, your reputation earns you your fee. What I mean is, even with modern bill levels being what they are, cases like this earn you enough to live for several months. Will you just put it toward living expenses?"

I shrug. "A chunk of it will go toward paying a few bills upfront, so I don't have to worry if I hit a dry spell since work is hit and miss for me when it comes to payouts. The rest is put aside so I can buy equipment I need and pay off the mortgage on my apartment. They have a good deal there where, for a small monthly fee, I still get the maintenance and security stuff tenants have, but with the security of not having to worry about potential eviction. This case *may* put me within touching distance, depending on how the place gets valued."

"That makes sense. It's a practical goal. And helps with the paranoia. If you're close, would Lori lend you the money for the rest?"

"Not that it's any of your business, but she already offered, and I refused. I don't take handouts, especially from a partner."

"My apologies. I knew you had a limit somewhere in terms of subjects for discussion."

I laugh. "And *I* knew *you* had a limit in terms of how well you could read me. That was my well-practiced serious face. You learn to make it look real in this line of work. Don't worry, I *am* taking the case seriously. You're afraid, though. It's good to relax at times like that."

"CAW."

"Gentle, Bert."

Thud.

I sit up, the solid whack of a metal gargoyle's beak on my forehead dragging me out of the blissful darkness of a surprisingly dreamless sleep.

"That was hardly what I would call gentle," Dr. Faraday says, her hushed voice the definition of exasperation.

I rub my eyes. "What's going on?"

"I'm not sure," Faraday replies. "One moment, Bert was fine, the next he was getting flustered and tapping on your phone."

"Ow," I say, rubbing where Bert took the drastic measure to wake me. Then, with the cobwebs beginning to clear, it dawns on me. I reach over the edge of the couch and fumble for my phone. "Good call on keeping the lights off. If this is what I think it is, you'll want to lay low."

I find the phone and immediately notice a blue light flashing at the top of the darkened screen. "A blue light means my security system back at the office is going off. Mind if I cast it to the TV?"

Faraday nods and turns the television on. I hold the cast button on the phone screen and flick the handset out toward the newly illuminated television screen, and we are immediately treated to a shot of the elusive stalker wandering around my apartment. After a few seconds, they lift the tablet in their hand and turn to face the security camera in the middle of the ceiling. Of course, their face is fully censored, so I don't get to confirm my suspicions just yet. A few taps on the tablet later, and we can see the message, *Good guess with Castleford.*

A few more taps, and now the message reads, *You're on the right track.*

More taps. *Come and get me.*

The stalker walks off screen and I tap to change cameras. I can see they're now sitting on *my* couch, arms crossed behind their head in a relaxed fashion.

"They're baiting me," I say. "And it's not like I have much choice but to do as they want. Keep the door locked. Bert, you stay here, just in case."

"Caw."

Dr. Faraday hugs herself, fear crawling all over her. "Will you be okay?"

I shrug, draw my Glock, and check it's loaded. "After I'm done with them, who knows? Let's see how far I can push the suitable force rules."

THE DRIVE BACK to my apartment doesn't take as long as it normally would. The combination of the lack of traffic along certain roads at this time of night and my own lack of regard for speed limits under the circumstances make sure of that. When I make it up to my floor, I find my door is still cracked open. One kick later, and I'm striding in, gun trained straight ahead at...an empty room.

Two large steps in and I can see down in front of the couch. There's nowhere to hide and nobody trying. Being in no mood to screw around, I state, "Lights on, all rooms," and the whole place is lit up instantly.

Keeping my gun ready, I move forward and give the bathroom a quick once-over. Empty.

"Which leaves the bedroom," I mutter, and step quickly across to the last room. From the open doorway I can tell nobody is in the far corner, so I step in and turn, adjusting my aim to behind the door.

Also empty.

Frowning, I pull my wardrobe doors open, step back, and aim.

Also empty.

Confused now, I start to run things through in my head at speed.

They got the censorship software into my systems but didn't even bother trying to turn the security system off. Because they wanted to send me a message. Wait. There are three cameras in the main room alone, yet they knew exactly which one to look at to make sure I saw it. They must be monitoring the whole system. But how?

The original video file. It's stored on my server, but I edited it down on the tablet and viewed it on my phone. Which means they must both be...

"*Diu*! The tracker in my car was a red herring to distract me from me considering how deep their software goes. They're already on their way to Faraday."

I holster the Glock and start to run back through my apartment. Just as I reach the door, a familiar voice says, "Hey."

I clench my fist and turn to shoot an angry glare at a man who looks *exactly* like my father. He smiles the same smile he gave me countless times through my life and says, "Keep digging, firecracker."

I turn away and growl, "And now I know," and then take off back toward my car, pausing only long enough to hit the speed dial for Devin Carmichael.

Chapter Six

BY THE TIME the elevator stops on Dr. Faraday's floor, I've just about regained my breath. The combination of the rush and my anger right now—both at the stalker and at myself—have left me feeling somewhat unfit. I run up the hall, turn the corner, and dash to my client's apartment. The door is open, hanging loosely.

Glock ready, I step inside and survey the carnage. The couch has been flipped and several broken glasses litter the floor. There are scratches in the floor and up one of the walls. Chairs have been thrown across the room and the door to the balcony is open. There's also an envelope stuck to the glass.

Scanning the room while I walk, I make my way over and grab the envelope, giving the balcony a quick glance while I do so. Inside it is a key marked with the label "7(5)." *Apartment seven, fifth floor. That's back by the elevator.*

"Well, that's clearly a trap. Where the hell are you, Bert?" I make a snap decision, look right up at the security camera, and say, "Okay, fine. I'll play your game."

With the key in hand, I steel myself and run to apartment seven. Not wanting to give them any prior warning, I slam the key into place, raise my gun, and boot the door open. The first thing I notice is Dr. Faraday and Bert, sitting on chairs, facing me. They aren't moving, aren't making any sound, they're just pointed toward the door. The second thing I notice is the body on the floor in front of them. He's lying face up with a visible cut running along his throat. From the lack of flowing blood, he's obviously not been alive for a little while. The third thing I notice is the feeling of a gun barrel pressed against the back of my head.

The slight increase in pressure is enough to make it clear what they want, so I let them guide me into the room from behind. Once I hear the door shut, I say, "Nurse Bridges. Or do you prefer Angel Tanner?"

"Very good," she replies. "Drop the gun."

The training Lori and I have been doing with Lt. Hanson has been interesting. She's been going through some basic self-defense with Lori, but she's also been throwing in some things that are a little more advanced. Such as ways to disarm an attacker with a weapon. More specifically, guns and knives.

I release the Glock from my hand, letting it clatter to the floor. Moving with as much speed as I can, I thrust my head to the side, then twist toward Tanner so our bodies are square to each other, and hook one arm around Tanner's gun arm. I swing a hard strike into her shoulder with my other hand, then grab the gun and force it into the wall behind her. She releases her grip on the firearm, but immediately twists her body toward me, grabs my arm, and throws me over her shoulder.

My back slams against the wall, then the room slips by as I crash headfirst onto the floor. I scramble to my feet just in time to see Tanner snatch my Glock from the floor and point it at my face. "Don't make me kill you. You're my preferred option right now."

"Preferred option, eh? And what does that mean?"

"In time." She waves the gun, and I follow the movement, circling into the room while Tanner mirrors me. "I want you to check the back of the machines' heads. You'll find a small metal box on each. If you don't want them to need rebuilding, *do not* try to remove them."

I back up and look down, finding the boxes just as she said. "What are they?"

"Remote disablers. Play ball and I'll deactivate them. Try something stupid, and I'll fry them. It's a simple choice."

I nod toward the body. "And him?"

Angel Tanner shoots me the same manic grin she did in the hospital during the LV case. "He was an acquaintance of a mutual acquaintance."

"I seriously doubt we walk in the same circles."

"You'd be surprised. Degrees of separation, and all that."

I shake my head. "Okay, so why's he dead?"

"There are very few things I detest in this life. Betrayal is one of them. There are plenty of things I love, though. Money, knowledge. Slowly toying with prey. *Especially* when they don't know what I'm planning."

I smile. "And that's what this is? You toying with me?"

"Not at all. Like I said, you're my preferred option for what's ahead. Now"—she waves the gun again—"get moving. We're going to make some house calls."

ANGEL TANNER LEADS me to the elevator and positions herself slightly behind me. The barrel of the Glock remains pressed into my lower back. "You know how this works. We reach the ground floor, and we keep walking, nice and casual. Try to raise the alarm, and I pull the trigger. Try to run, and I pull the trigger. You kept this thing loaded, right?"

"Unfortunately."

The elevator lets out a *ding*, and the door opens to the ground floor. We walk out into the main lobby and I spot one of the guards Dr. Faraday introduced me to. He nods my way and says, "Miss Tam."

"Hey," I reply.

"Everything okay?"

We keep walking. "Yeah," I say as we pass. "Just heading out to follow up a lead for the Doc."

He nods. "Well, good luck. I hope you manage to sort this mess out soon."

"Me too."

We make it to my car. Tanner pats the driver's side door. "You get in. Don't even think about trying to drive off without me."

"I wouldn't dream of skipping out on such good company."

I sit in the driver's seat, and Tanner climbs into the back seat. She pats the side of my head with the gun, and I sneer at her.

"Temper, temper, detective. Now, drive."

"Drive where?"

"Twenty-three Lambert Drive."

I put the car in gear and pull out into the street, confusion etched on my face. "I know that address."

"Good. Means you won't get us lost."

"Funny."

Tanner lets out a cackle and relaxes back into her seat. She makes a point of noisily checking the magazine, so I know I'm still expected to follow orders. "You know the address because the owner once hired you to track down his daughter. It was quite a high-profile case, in the end."

"Jonah Burrell?"

"Exactly."

"Why? Why him?"

"Oh, don't worry. Jonah is *not* the main event. This is more of a social call, for old times' sake. Plus, I thought you may find it all quite interesting."

"Sounds like the two of you go way back."

"I wouldn't want to spoil the surprise. Less talk, more drive."

The rest of the journey, as short as it is, feels like it takes forever. The combination of silence, the knowledge my passenger has a gun pointed at me, and the simple fact I have no idea how to swing the odds back in my favor will do that.

When we reach Lambert Drive, I instantly remember how fancy an area it is when compared to my part of the city. There are only four houses here, and they're pretty big. They're numbered twenty-one to twenty-four, and nobody knows why. Rumor has it, when the city was built, this was supposed to be a bigger street, but I can't say I buy that. Right now, I'm more concerned with the question "why?" Why are we here? Why is Jonah Burrell waiting outside his open front door? And why does he look so tired?

I park the car and step out, Angel Tanner moving in synch behind me. "Jonah," I say.

He nods to me and then shifts his gaze to Angel. For a moment, he just stares. Then, he turns and walks back inside.

Angel nudges me with the gun, and I follow him into the house. We all enter his study, and he points us to some comfy-looking leather chairs. Tanner guides me into one, grabs a wooden chair from the back wall, and sits down behind me. I don't need to turn around to know the gun is still trained on my head.

Jonah sits tiredly into the chair opposite me and stares at Angel. "It was you, wasn't it? The hallucinations. They were holograms."

"I prefer the term projected memories," she says.

"Memories. Yes. It must have taken months to recreate them."

Angel Tanner laughs. "Is that what you think? It seems I misunderstood who you are here. Well, well. I guess Cassie isn't the only one who's going to learn things tonight."

Jonah looks at me and says, "I am truly sorry about all this."

I sigh. "Don't worry about it. It's not like I've never been in this sort of situation before."

"Oh, you've skirted around the edges before now," Angel says. "But this will be new, even for you. Now, let's get on with it. Jonah, why don't you tell the good detective *what* I am."

"Sadistic," he replies. "Insane."

"Your biggest mistake?" she tries. "You know full well what I mean, Jonah. I had the decency to tell you I was coming so you could send your family away for the evening. I did it to make this easier for you. Do not misunderstand my intentions, though. I have no love for them. If you don't do what I want, when I want it, I *will* find them. Do you know what *hallucinations* you'll be seeing every night then?"

The color drains from Jonah's face. He keeps his eyes on Angel but addresses me. "She's a Familiar Unit. Hybrid Programming, just like Angela and Bert."

"Angela?" I ask.

"Dr. Faraday. You met her during Bert's last major repair session."

I nod back over my shoulder. "That one's been stalking her. She hired me to find out who the stalker was. The paperwork she filled in just stated Dr. Faraday as her identifier. I was beginning to think she didn't have a first name. Still, at least now I know what the third hybrid unit is."

"The first, technically. I built Angel years before I came to New Hopeland."

"Tell the detective *why* you built me," Angel cuts in.

He sighs and rests his head in his hands. "Because I could."

"Because. He. Could. You hear that? I was built on a whim. Without a purpose. And that's the thing, isn't it? Some people do things just because. But others, they work with purpose. Take you, for example. You work your cases; you help your clients. Why? Because you think it's the right thing to do. Because you stand, not with those in control, but with the people of New Hopeland. That's what you told Devin Carmichael, isn't it?"

I stand up and turn to face her, my eyes narrowed. "How did you know that?"

"Hmm. How indeed? The same way I know you have your suspicions about how I know any of the things I've taken advantage of. And now I know," she says, mimicking my voice from back in my apartment. "That's what you said. It was the firecracker comment, wasn't it? I thought it may not be true, but I used it anyway. I wanted you to know you were right. But the overall picture is far bigger than you thought.”

“Meaning?”

Tanner glances toward Jonah and shakes her head. “No. I already overplayed Jonah’s part in this. There’s no need to discuss this in front of him. Here’s an interesting little tidbit for you. The police have had several opportunities to kill me back home but haven’t. The reason is someone here figured out what I was. That’s why Jonah came to New Hopeland. I was put on some sort of ‘do not kill’ list.”

“How did you know that?” Jonah asks, his voice now tinged with fear.

“I can see *everything* now, Jonah. There are no secrets I cannot just sift through at will. At least as far as *you’re* concerned. And a few others, of course.”

“The King’s Guard,” I say.

“Yes. Like I was told you were. I will hold my hands up in defeat on that one. They tricked me. Had I been in the position then that I am in now, it would have taken a lot more work. Now, though, I know the truth. Or part of it, anyway.”

“You know,” Jonah says, “you’re right it was your existence that landed me my main contracts here. And you *are* on the ‘do not kill’ list as far as California goes. Angela is important to my client, and to kill you there would risk exposure of her existence in an uncontrolled manner. Now you’re in New Hopeland, I’m not so sure the list applies. Here, they could cover up what happened. What you are. Really, you would do better to just leave.”

“Oh, I will. Eventually.” She giggles and shakes her head. “I could always tell when you were lying, Jonah. So, tell me truthfully. Do you know what your client wants to do with my fellow creation?”

"No. No, I don't. I just get instructions and follow them."

"And you do it not just for the pay, but because you enjoy the work." Angel uses the Glock to scratch her head. "So, my life is in danger by being here. Well then, I best get this all over with, hadn't I? You, detective, may not be King's Guard, but you *do* have a link to Allen Fuerza. Take out your phone and call him."

I have no other option but to comply. So, I slowly grip my phone, making sure to hit the button to hang up my current call. Then, I slide it out of my pocket, scroll to Fuerza's name in my contacts, and dial. While the phone rings, Angel walks closer and jabs the gun into my ribs. Eventually, he picks up. "Cassandra Tam. To what do I owe the pleasure?"

Angel reaches around my shoulder and pulls the phone closer to her own face. "Hey, kid. Wanna join your father?"

"You," he replies. Were it not for the current circumstances, I'd smile at the unexpected surprise in his voice.

"Me. Roll out the welcome carpet. I'm bringing the detective for a little visit. You may bring one guest only. It can even be that guy with the scar if you like. Any more than the four of us in the building, though, and the underground finds out exactly what I know." She hangs up and says, "Let's get going. You know where he'll meet us. Oh, and Jonah? Don't call the cops."

We leave the house and head back to my car. Once we're inside, I start the engine and Angel says, "He was a victim, you know. The first, in fact. I needed to check my theory about the blood, and he seemed like a good target to practice on. Fathers are supposed to help their daughters after all."

I frown. "During the LV case, you mean? He wasn't on the victim list."

"He wouldn't go the police. He was afraid they'd think he was insane."

"So, how does the blood figure into all of this?"

"First, Casille. Then, *maybe* I'll tell you. This won't end tonight, detective. But depending how this meeting plays out, I will at least know if I'm playing with a loaded gun, or if I need to rethink my strategy."

I pull out into the empty road and ask, "If you're that uncertain, then why put yourself at risk by meeting him like this? You know who he'll bring with him; you already mentioned the guy with the scar. I call him Sunglasses. He's not someone you want to get on the wrong side of."

"Sunglasses. Cute. His real name is Ethan Cobalt, if you were wondering. Though, if truth be told, I do have my doubts about that little snippet of information. But yes, I know who he is and what he's capable of. I may even know a little more than you with regards to that one. If all goes well, I'll know *a lot* more soon enough. As it is, I know enough to be certain *he* won't try to kill me, not tonight."

"I'm guessing you know where Casille's main base of operations is already, then?"

"Yes, so don't try to stall for time or take me somewhere else." She prods the gun in the back of my head, then clarifies, "The warehouses near the Government Monitoring Offices."

I take a right, driving carefully. The roads are pretty empty at the moment, but I want to buy myself some time. And give Devin a chance to get a clear shot at her. After my call, he should have been tracking me. If he heard everything that was said at Jonah's, he'll also know who we're heading to meet. My hope is he's finding somewhere to set up with a clear view of the floor we'll be visiting. "I don't get it," I say. "Half the time, you sound like you know exactly what you're doing. The rest of the time, you seem to be taking blind chances. Like the loaded gun comment when you had my Glock."

She jabs the gun hard into my ribs, and it scrapes a little along my back. It feels like she bruised me. "This one's loaded; I know that for certain."

"Is that a nice way of telling me to shut up?"

She laughs. "Not at all. I like your curiosity. Your Glock was a calculated risk. It's still back here, by the way. Feel free to recover it when this is all done. As to what I *do* know?" She pauses, and I see her glance out the window in the rearview mirror. "There are reasons I can't give the game away just yet. I am a gambling woman, detective. But I do not take pointless risks. I know enough to be certain of *this* course of action. How it plays out will decide the *next* course of action. Pull in over here."

I obediently park the car and wait for further instructions from my captor. She looks around and says, "Good. Now, open the door and step out. Slowly. I want you standing with your back to me, hands behind your head."

I do as I'm told, and hear Angel do the same. She pushes the rear door shut, does the same with my driver's door, and orders, "Okay, let's go. Keep your hands where they are."

We walk straight to the door and I push it open. *No sign of Devin. Either he's not here yet or he's waiting until we're up in the main room.*

Once the door swings shut, Angel says, "Stop. Okay, keeping your arms where they are, relax your elbows a little. I want as many potential angles as possible if I have to shoot."

"Great," I respond. "Oh, Miss Tam, is it? And what do you do for a living exactly? Why, I'm a human shield, of course. I'm easy to hide behind, and I have all these convenient gaps to work as shooting angles. The pay's awful, but the excitement more than makes up for it."

Tanner snorts behind me and replies, "You're masking. You don't need to be afraid. If I intended to kill you, I'd have done it already, and trust me, *I'm* going to be their focus."

"And I'm going to be in the way. I'm also expendable."

"Aww, such a low opinion of yourself. If only you knew. Now, don't move. We wait for them to come to get us. It's a little thing, but I want Casille to know who's in charge here. He's at my beck and call, not the other way around."

And so, we wait. *At least it gives Devin more time.*

After a long, slow minute, Sunglasses enters through the door at the back of the room. In a wonderful show of defiance, he simply looks at us and says, "Miss Tam, Miss Tanner. This way," then turns and walks back through the door.

"I'll give him that one," Tanner mutters and shoves me, just above where she bruised my back in the car. "Get moving."

"A please wouldn't hurt," I grumble and move toward the door, arms still in place. We follow the one scary Paloma I've ever met all the way up to Allen Fuerza's normal meeting room. Even now, he's still insistent on sitting on that ridiculous throne of his. We move across the room, and Sunglasses says, "That's quite close enough. Miss Tam, I don't suppose you could move, could you?"

"Move anywhere other than where I say, and I blow your brains out."

I sigh at Angel's words and respond, "I don't think I can, no."

"It's fine," Casille says, watching us from his seat. "It has been a *very* long time, Angel."

"Yes, it has, hasn't it? Did you follow my instructions? I kept them simple enough. Only the two of you, and the two of us in the building?"

Casille waves a hand as though he were playing the overconfident Allen Fuerza, and says, "Yes, yes. Though I do question why you bought the good detective here with you?"

"Oh, that's your fault, Casille. See, I know she's not King's Guard now. But she was a pawn, so I thought I may as well use her a little myself. I hope you don't mind. In fact, let's get her position in this all cleared up. Cassie, why don't you go ahead and tell dear Casille how you ended up in this mess?"

I roll my eyes. "I was hired to track down a stalker. Turned out it was Angel here. She's also been targeting a few people on the King's Guard list *you* supplied her with. I don't know what dirt she has on you all, but if she's been doing the same thing to everyone, she's digging up things from their past and using holographic projectors to make them relive stuff they really don't want to. Honestly, I wouldn't normally mind, you can all play whatever sick little games you want with each other, but I'm pretty sure I'm not the only non-King's Guard on the list she's targeting. Oh, and Malcolm Castleford is dead. But I assume you knew that already, eh?"

"Yes, that was unfortunate," Casille replies. "I had high hopes for him in a way. It was Harold Sanderson who killed him, if you were wondering."

"And," Angel cuts in, "he's more than prepared for any retaliation you may attempt. I think you'll find old Harry is far harder to kill than that runt Castleford was. Or your father, for that matter."

A look of anger shoots across Casille's face, but he buries it quickly. "What do you want, Angel?"

"Oh, that's simple. I just want you to know."

"To know?"

"Yes. To know I'm still here, and I have enough information to start putting things in action." She chuckles. "Do you know what I loathe, Casille? Betrayal. That was why your father died. He found out what I was and went to some very powerful people. People he believed he could trust, but who were just as intent on using him as I was. It's funny really, don't you think? Of course, you were always supposed to join him in the grave, but you disappeared before I could make it happen. Once I realized you were *here*, and more precisely, what you're doing...well, I couldn't help but dig a little. That was when I found the detective's client, Dr. Faraday. You know who she is, right?"

"We know who she is," Sunglasses replies, "and indeed, *what* she is. That is what you really wanted to know, is it not?"

"Indeed," she mocks. "Well now, that confirms what I needed to know. This whole city is a betrayal. A betrayal of so, so many people. I'm going to make good use of this meeting, Casille. Mark my words."

Bang.

The gunshot cuts through the night, and the bullet cuts cleanly through the window to my left. It rushes by me, and I hear it *thud* against the wall to my right. *He missed?*

"Very good. You did *exactly* as I expected. I will deactivate the disablers and leave my dear sister alone," Angel says. "And Casille? I will watch your city burn. Sweet dreams, kid."

Casille rises to his feet. "She's gone?"

I turn and see he's right. "What happened?"

Sunglasses steps forward and takes something off my back. He holds it out and turns it over in his hand a few times. Before he can say anything, my cell phone rings. It's Devin. I hit answer, and he says, "Hey, Caz, put me on speaker, would ya?"

I do so, and Casille says, "Mr. Carmichael. Good shooting, as always."

"Yeah, well, if you hadn't given me access to the cameras, I wouldn't have been able to line it up at all. She weren't showing up on the thermal. Hologram?"

"It seems so," Sunglasses says. "Miss Tam had a small projector on her back. It's lightweight, but the speaker is decent. It's not a model I'm familiar with."

"*Diu.* When did she put that on me?"

"It could have been any time really. The question is, how long has it been running?"

I blink. "She physically shoved me when you came to get us. She must have put it on me then. But that means he might still be..."

The roar of an engine cuts in and we all turn to look in its direction. After a moment, Devin says, "Motorcycle, heading out and into the city. She probably had it stashed here earlier."

"Which means there's a mole," Casille says. "Well. There's nothing we can do about her right now, is there? Can I leave that to you?"

Sunglasses nods, knowing the question was directed toward him. Then, he looks to me and says, "It was a wise decision to get Devin involved. You do not disappoint, Miss Tam."

I scowl at him. "I really hope this wasn't some elaborate plan of yours?"

"No, pure happenstance in this case. For that, I apologize."

"Yeah? Like I said, I wasn't the only one caught in the crossfire this time. Check the King's Guard list. There's at least one cop on there who got hit."

"A cop?"

"Lieutenant Hanson. She's a friend of mine. I'd rather you kept people I actually like out of this mess."

"Noted," he replies.

"Oh, and Caz?" I look down at my phone, and Devin continues, "No charge for tonight. Technically, I missed."

He hangs up, and I look back to Casille and Sunglasses. "Can I go now? I need to get back to my client."

"Of course," Casille replies. "If you hear anything useful, let us know. We'll do the same."

I MAKE IT back to the room where I'd left Dr. Faraday and Bert relatively quickly and find Angel kept her word. Both are already back in action and dealing with a member of the local police.

"You expect me to believe you were taken here and the body was already there? Is there any evidence of this stalker investigation?" he asks Faraday, just as I walk in.

"Yes, there is," I cut in. "Cassandra Tam, PI. I've been running the investigation."

"Do you have a case license? Stalker cases are complex here."

I nod and pull out my cell phone, load up the license, and hand it over. "You new here?" I try.

"Yes, he is." Cpl. Devereaux enters the room and places a hand on the guy's shoulder. "Tam works *with* us, not against us, Roberts. I was the same when I first met her. You get used to her, though."

I smile. "Get used to me, eh? I'm not that bad."

"Not always."

"The license checks out," Roberts says, handing back the phone.

"Which means you know what's going on here," I say. "With all due respect, my client has been through a traumatic few days. Unless you have any direct questions for her, I would like to escort her back to her room. I'll be making my official report tomorrow, and I'm sure Miss Faraday would be happy to make herself available for further questioning once she's had a chance to rest and process the evening's events."

Roberts starts to protest, but Devereaux cuts him off. "Do you have any follow-up questions or not?"

"None. If she was involved, we'll find evidence here anyway."

"Exactly. It's a safe bet Bert there will have recorded everything, too, so we'll have plenty to go on. So, Tam, you go ahead and get Miss Faraday back home. It's just up the hall, right? The room with the damaged door?" She nods, and he continues. "The building staff have put it back in place. I'm afraid the room is still a mess, though."

"Come on," I say. "I'll help put it back together. Bert, this way."

"Caw," Bert says, and hops off the table he's been sitting on waiting for commands. He clambers up my leg and onto my shoulder, and we all make our way back to Faraday's apartment.

While we tidy, I fill her in on the important events: Jonah knows what happened, Angel Tanner was the stalker, and while she escaped, she did promise to leave her alone. I didn't tell her Angel is the third hybrid Familiar. While understandably freaked out, Dr. Faraday agreed the likelihood of Angel breaking her word right now was low, especially as she'd reactivated both her fellow Hybrid Familiars, just as she promised. Once the tidying was done, we parted ways with the added stipulation that I'd be on call if we turned out to be wrong.

I ARRIVE HOME late, and immediately start searching for the projector Angel used to show me my father. Having seen the one she attached to my back, I at least know what to look for. In the end, I find it on my ceiling. It takes dragging my worktable across the room and standing on it to get it down.

Sunglasses was right that it's lightweight, and the speaker worked well enough to fool us all. With a sigh, I sit back into my slightly uncomfortable work chair and toss the projector onto the table. Which is when two things happen. First, all the lights in the block go out. Second, the device springs into life. A light flashes above it, and a life-size projection of Angel Tanner's smiling face appears, floating above the table.

"Well, that's not creepy at all. You've been a vampire, and masked stalker, and now...what? The Dullahan?"

To my surprise, the face replies, "I hadn't thought of that one. And yes, the power cut is me. I needed the cameras off for this."

"Uh huh. All I really care about is whether you're going to keep your word and leave my client alone."

"Absolutely. I've satisfied my curiosity with her, for now, at least. I'll find out everything there is to know about my dear sister when I'm done dealing with Casille, anyway. I do believe you're lying to me, though."

"Am I?"

"Yes, you are. You're itching to know what's going on in the city. That much was obvious from the file notes you had on me. By the way, secure servers aren't what they seem. If I've seen it, so have others. Oh, and your phone has a slight delay."

"A slight delay," I repeat, letting the words out slowly.

"Oh yes. It was quite annoying. You see, I have access to some government level stuff right now. I had an earpiece in when we visited Jonah. I could hear you in the room and through the earpiece via your *secret call* to Devin Carmichael. Smart move given the information you had, not so much if you'd known how much gets monitored in this city."

I sit in silence for a moment, then respond. "What do you want?"

"The question is what do *you* want, Cassie? I tell you what. When you found me, there was a body. I told you he was an acquaintance of a mutual acquaintance. If you want to find out what's going on in this city, then find out who our mutual acquaintance is. They'll tell you what you need to do to get back in touch with me. If I don't hear from you within two weeks, then I'll assume you're either not interested or you're supremely overrated. Either way,

I won't hold your attempt to have me killed against you, and you'll only hear from me directly regarding what happens next if you want to."

And with that, the projector shuts down and the apartment block's power returns. "I should have used the ping box," I grumble.

"Caw," Bert agrees.

A SUDDEN WETNESS causes me to screw my eyes shut even tighter than they already are. The rain battering my face is too much, though, and soon enough, I dip my head forward and wipe my eyes with my surprisingly warm fingers. When I finally force my eyes open, I find I'm standing in the middle of a field.

No, not really a field. Look around you. There are gravestones everywhere. This is an old, pre-virtual cemetery. Which means you're dreaming.

Looking around me, I can see it's nighttime. The moon is full and visible between the mass of dark clouds busy pouring water down on me. It's strange; I can feel each drop hitting me, but they don't have a discernible temperature. They aren't cold or warm, they just *are*. I sigh and start to walk forward, following the gaps between each stone. They're all blank, nameless slabs.

Up ahead, a movement catches my eye. I spot Angel Tanner weaving silently through the stones, much the same as I am.

You know how your dreams work by now. Follow her and see what you missed.

Never one to disobey the commands of my occasionally bossy inner monologue, I speed up and play follow the leader until Angel disappears around the back of a tree. When I notice that she doesn't emerge around the other side, I slow my pace and proceed with a little more caution. Even then, I'm not surprised to find she has already vanished when I pass beyond the hulking mass of wood. I can't say I was expecting to find a single gravestone in the middle of an eerily lit clearing, though.

Much like the rest, there's no inscription on the stone. Other than its location, the thing that sets this one apart is the grave itself is open. Peering in, I can see a coffin partially exposed below, and a shovel sticking out of the remaining soil. Figuring the hint is fairly obvious, I lower myself down into the hole and proceed to grab the shovel and get to work.

The grave isn't too deep, so it's not too difficult to scoop up large amounts of dirt and place it up on ground level. In truth, uncovering the coffin doesn't take too long. The problem is each pile of dirt is accompanied by a short, sharp blast of pain in my head, and a rapid-fire burst of memory. The time my refusal to let a closed case stay on the finished list led to me effectively ending a marriage due to uncovering an infidelity unrelated to the case itself. Leaning against the inside of Charlie's front door, trying to keep an angry drunk out who was intent on giving me a physical response to my revealing his financial flights of fancy. Times I've caught the bad guys but caused distress to those who hired me. Or who cared for me. Who I cared for.

Eventually, I scrape the last of the dirt away and find myself staring at the uncovered coffin. Opening it up is a little awkward given I'm standing on top of the thing, but with a little clever wedging of my legs against opposite sides of the pit, I'm able to lift the lid enough to drop my feet down just under the wooden slab and push it fully open. To my disappointment, it's empty, bar one more flash of the past. The moment a trigger was pulled five times, and my dad...

I shake it away and stare up at the sky, watching my breathe rise from my mouth, creating an illusion of coldness. After a moment, I place my hands back up on the grassy ground above and haul myself up and out of the hole, and onto my knees. As I sit up, I spot that something has changed. The gravestone is no longer blank, but now simply displays a name. I grimace and read it out loud to myself.

"Cassandra Tam."

I DON'T KNOW whether the end of the dream was when I woke up, or if I drifted into a dreamless state afterward, but the next thing I see is the light creeping in through my Venetian blinds. With how tired I was last night, I forgot to set an alarm.

Which is fine. Today is going to be a long one, because even if I know far too well what the dream meant, there are some things I can't just leave alone.

Resolute in my path, I slowly make my way through my morning routine: eating the same breakfast as normal, taking the same length of time in the shower, and changing into the same clothing selection of neat trousers, white shirt, and black tie. Most of what remains of today is going to be work related, after all.

Once Bert is powered down and on charge, I make my way to my first destination: the police station. Once my paperwork is filed, I request a meeting with the marshal of the PD's Tech Shifter Division, Donal O'Brien. The burly Irishman is happy to oblige, and walks over to offer a firm handshake and a hearty, "Cassie, how are ya?"

I return both the handshake and the smile, and reply, "Could be worse. Did you hear what happened?"

"Aye. I'm glad you're okay, and you're keeping in *their* good books. It's a tough path you're on."

"Don't I know it. I just wanted to pass on a concern, and you seemed like the best person to speak to."

"Oh?"

"Remember how during the LV case you told me the only people on the victim list with direct connections to the Kings were Joe Farrah, Jack Stan, and Pauline Mensche? Well, Joe got targeted during this. So did Hanson. Are you certain she wasn't one of the fake King's Guard on the list Castleford sent Tanner's way?"

"She certainly wasn't a fake King's Guard, no. Castleford could have gone off list, I suppose, but there's no way to check now. I think she had some *dealings* in California way back, though. Maybe Tanner was picking up on an old grudge Hanson hasn't mentioned?"

Given how Angel Tanner seems to deal with her grudges, it seems unlikely. Hmm.

"Maybe." I put my hands in my pockets and ask, "Did they clear up the mess with the body in the apartment? That new guy seemed pretty certain I was the killer."

Donal laughs, "Yeah, Dev said Roberts was on the war path. He'll calm down eventually, I'm sure. Last I heard you were in the clear, though it's not like Roberts didn't try to piece anything together."

"Am I going to have to hit him?"

"Ya never know. It was a weak link, anyway. The guy was named Frank Tyson, and he was one of the contributors to that conspiracy website you helped us shut down, *The Roots of Eden are Rotten*. He avoided jail time because he cut a deal to hand over the details of a bunch of stuff Gary Locke was up to. Roberts decided that, as you were responsible for Locke's arrest, you must have gotten pissed and took matters into your own hands when Tyson was set free."

I roll my eyes. "Someone's desperate to make an impact, eh?"

"Well, he's certainly done that. You'll be happy to know your reputation is good enough that he's landed with a crash on the fair-game-to-ride-mercilessly list."

At that, I smile. "Good to know. I'm tempted to visit Locke now, just to wind Roberts up. Well, I better head out. I need to check in with my client."

"Fair enough. Stay safe."

I turn and walk away, waving my acknowledgement as I retreat to my car to head to my second stop, the FE Limited offices. In a way, I didn't lie. I *am* checking on my now former client to a degree, but it's not Dr. Faraday I'm meeting with.

By the time I reach his office, Jonah Burrell is pacing in and out of the door waiting for me. Looking at him, I doubt he's slept much, if at all. He beckons me inside and immediately pours himself a whiskey, leaving me to shut the door behind us. He downs it and pours another, then offers, "Drink?"

I shake my head. "No, I better not. I still have some errands to run today, and I'm going to need to be able to drive. Spirits knock me out pretty quickly."

He nods and sits down, nursing his new drink as he regards me. "I really don't know why my client wanted me to build Angela, and I really can't tell you who they are, you know."

I take the seat opposite him and reply, "I know. Honestly, I don't care about that. I was more..." I take a moment to consider my words, and Jonah waits patiently for me to collect myself. Finally, I decide how to continue. "Angel Tanner is a cold, calculating killer. She has a predisposition for violence and manipulation. She's also programmed the same way as Dr. Faraday. And Bert."

Relief drifts over Jonah's face. "Ah. You're worried about them."

"Yes. I want to know if they're going to turn out the same as Angel Tanner."

Jonah takes another sip and rubs his chin. "Were it not for Angel, they may have. It's the way the programming interacts. Essentially, the system builds bonds between different simulated stimuli. The pre-built potential of violence in the Protector class tends to get entangled with the positive reinforcement aspects of the Family class. Honestly, I don't know why."

"But it escalates."

"It did with Angel because she was left unchecked. It's different for both Angela and Bert."

I cross my arms. "How is it different?"

"Angela was built with a naturally suspicious streak, designed to feed into an interest in conspiracy theories. That was actually requested by the client but was an ideal way for me to funnel the potential negatives into something more mundane."

"You're telling me she won't end up like Angel Tanner because she has a hobby?"

"That's a rather simplified version of it, but essentially, yes. And Bert, he has an outlet. Your job means he is given a means to let it all out in a controlled and targeted manner."

I take that in, and nod. "That makes sense. How certain are you, though? In both cases."

"Almost one hundred percent. Angel wasn't always the way she is, she just grew to view power as important and criminals as powerful. I think her first murder probably pushed her over the edge. Or solidified her chosen path for her at least."

"And machines are harder to stop than people."

"In some cases. Both Angel and Angela are built with human limitations. Unless Angel found a way to modify herself, she's no more difficult to *stop* than any human with her level of influence."

"Then why didn't you do something about her before she ended up controlling California?"

He smiles sadly and stares into his drink, slowly sloshing it from side to side. "I didn't know until she actually killed someone. And then? Part of me wanted to fix her, to make it right. I just didn't know how. So, I helped her cover the first one up. Everything escalated too quickly after that."

I sigh. "Okay. Okay, that...it's not what I expected, but...at least Bert isn't going to turn into her."

"No. I know you've had some concerns recently, but I checked the diagnostics myself. He's fine."

I take a deep breath and get to my feet. "Okay. Good. Look, I don't know what deal you're stuck in, but be careful, eh? For everyone's sake."

I turn and leave and make my way back to the car. Right now, something Angel Tanner said to me is running through my head. *If you'd known how much gets monitored in this city.*

I lean back in my car seat. "Even with *this*, I'm paranoid now. Still. Nothing I can do about that."

I grab my cell phone and hit the speed dial for Lori. When she picks up, I say, "Hey. Fancy going for a picnic?"

"AND THAT'S ABOUT all I can tell you."

"Wow. You sure you can't say more?"

"Sorry, client confidentiality, and all that."

Lori giggles. "I wasn't being serious. What you said was enough to worry me. Anything else and I don't know what I'd do."

I shift a little from my position lying next to Lori, resting my head on her lap to look up at her and smile. "Sorry."

She playfully flicks my nose. "And don't keep apologizing. I know what your job is like sometimes. First-hand, if you remember. As much as I worry about you, I'm with you by choice. I like the design on your tie today, by the way. What is it?"

"A cicada. It's supposed to represent immortality. Given I've survived two encounters with California's most wanted, it seemed appropriate, eh?"

Lori runs her fingers through my hair and smiles. "Don't you get cocky, Cassie Tam. That'll be the thing that...well."

"I'm joking," I reply, lifting a hand to stroke her cheek. She raises her own hand to mine, and pulls it across to kiss it, then lets it drop gently back to my lap.

"It's nice out here."

"Yeah. I know it's only a little way outside the city, but I kinda needed it. Way back, this was my little refuge if a case hit a little too close to home. I haven't been here for ages, but I always did like the scenery. All trees and quiet. Apart from the birds."

"Sounds like a pretty private thing to make me a part of. I feel honored."

"I'm being kinda selfish there, I think."

"Yeah?"

"Yeah. I really did want to see you, don't get me wrong, but I was also planning something else. I'm going to do something really stupid, and honestly, no matter how it goes, I'm gonna need support. It was kinda your idea, actually. And you know what they say, if someone throws you under a bus, make damn sure you drag them under with you...no, wait. That sounded way too crazy. Sorry."

Lori laughs out loud and grabs my hand, giving it a firm squeeze. "You're panicking. What are you up to?"

I reach into my pocket and pull out a piece of paper. "I couldn't even bring myself to add the number to my phone," I say, handing it to her.

Lori reads the name at the top of the little torn sheet, then hands it back to me with a smile. She leans down and kisses my forehead, and whispers, "I'm proud of you."

An apologetic tear forms in one eye, and I pull out my cell phone. I don't need to read the number again. It hasn't changed since before I left Vancouver—a quick check of the online phone registry confirmed that—and the digits are still locked tight in my memory. So, I type in the digits, hit dial, and wait.

Ring-ring.
Ring-ring.
Ring-click.
"Hello?"

I swallow hard and close my eyes, and Lori's hand tightens on mine. "Hi, Mom."

Script for AL Berry's Funeral Company Video Advert, Circa 2072

Advert for use on TV, streaming services, social media and the official company website.

VIDEO	AUDIO
SCENE 1	SCENE 1
Open with stock footage from news reports regarding lack of space in cemeteries. Clips run silently to allow voice over.	*Voice-over performed by Al Berry.* Ever since the Religious Group Land Crash (RGLC) of 2030, people have been searching for the best solution for their burial needs. That's where we come in.
SCENE 2	SCENE 2
Cut to the main waiting room at the Al Berry Funeral Company head office. Al Berry smiles and lays out the key points. During "POST" line, have the word appear on	*Al Berry now on screen.* Al Berry's Funeral Company has been at the forefront of the industry since before cremations became mandatory. The

screen animated, with the letters moving to line up vertically, and the meaning of each appearing as Al talks.	reason for that is simple: POST. Price, Options, Simplicity, Timeliness. Here Al Berry's Funeral Company, we don't believe in making things complicated. To that end, we offer only one package: the **complete package**. This includes the following services:
SCENE 3	**SCENE 3**
Animated scene to illustrate network capabilities, showing data travelling in a line across the globe in the form of a glowing light. Once the lights hit a VR headset, switch to silent clips of mock-up funerals. The footage from the website can be used here.	*Voice-over performed by Al Berry.* We will set up a virtual funeral, and using our worldwide network, make it easy for loved ones to attend from the comfort of their own home. Should they find themselves unable to attend on the day, the entire event will also be available retroactively via an interactive repeat. The only thing missing will be the inter-personal interactions that come with being there live.

SCENE 3a	SCENE 3a
New footage required. Create mock-up of mourner at memorial site using an access code, then getting alert relating to other mourners gaining access. Cut to split screen so that we can see the other mourner using a different code but ending up at an identical memorial site.	We will set up a virtual memorial site. This will be housed in a fully interactive environment, and will be available for use 24/7, all year round. All you'll need is the access code, and you can enter the area with **any** VR set, no matter the specs of the hardware. Best of all, our systems can run twenty separate versions of the room. This means that, when you log on, you'll be able to choose which room you use, ensuring you never have to meet your fellow mourners unless you want to. With all twenty versions being identical, nobody has to miss out on remembering their loved ones again!
SCENE 3b	SCENE 3b
The stock footage merges back into one shot and pans around to the memorial itself. This then cycles through a number	Our package comes with full personalization, as per the wishes of the next of kin, or the deceased in the event of specifications

of different options already available. Use most popular five at time of editing but cover five different religious practices.

set out in the Last Will and Testament. That means not only can we split the ashes to fit your need, we can facilitate your service and memorial requirement no matter what religion or belief system you follow. In fact, we are so confident in our services, that if we do not hold suitable presets in our databases, we will do two things.

One, we will cut your first fee by 15 percent.

Two, our design team will meet with you to ascertain your individual needs and create these for you as part of the package.

<u>SCENE 3c</u>	<u>SCENE 3c</u>

Here, show footage of the design team talking to a customer, and illustrate changes being made in real time on a computer screen.

Worried about the initial recovery of your loved ones remains? As per the UN's guidelines on the enforced disposal of bodies, we will even take

	care of the physical cremation for you. Using one of our state of the art, custom built facilities, we will ensure you receive your loved ones remains in a timely fashion, ready for you to store as you please.
<u>END SCENE 3</u>	
Cut to a shot of the newest Al Berry crematorium. Show from the outside during clear weather, then cut to shot of various urns in the display cabinet.	
<u>SCENE 4</u>	<u>SCENE 4</u>
Now we enter the money section. It is important to show a human face again hear, so we cut to Al Berry sat at his desk, talking pleasantly. Important note: keep the desk clear of general clutter but use "sympathy items" such as tissues and a multi-religion wreath	*Al Berry now on screen.* **Words in bold to be emphasized.** The question is, how much does this all cost? You will be happy to know that, as at time of filming, we remain the most competitively priced virtual funeral service in the world for the sheer

catalogue to flank him. In the background, display two framed certificates, one for the 2070 gold star customer satisfaction award, and one for the current official registration. This will aid in the viewer establishing a link between Al Berry's Funeral Company and concepts of sympathy, good service, following official guidelines, and variety.

number of customizations we offer.

As such, the whole package is available for a total of **only** $17,000. This fee includes everything listed above, **plus** the first three years hosting for the memorial site. Once the three years is up, you will have the option to renew for another three years at a **reduced cost** of $8,000.

Don't want to—or can't—renew? That's fine too! You will also have the option to purchase the memorial site for a **small one-off fee** of $3,500, effectively removing it from our servers but allowing it to be stored on your own systems. Still not affordable? Unless instructed otherwise, at the cessation of a payment agreement, we will store your memorial site on our systems for a total of ten years, giving you time to raise the

	funds to purchase or renew the plan. And remember, each purchased plan comes with our personal guarantee that you will receive the services offered within ten weeks of the full payment clearing into our accounts. If not? We'll refund 25 percent of the cost for each additional month it takes, right up to a total of 75 percent of the cost.
SCENE 4a	SCENE 4a
Here, display the e-mail address and company website in bold at the bottom of the screen. Small print at the bottom of the screen should read *"Note: Prices and terms of service correct at time of filming, but subject to change without warning."*	With prices like this, can you really afford not to leave your needs to us? To get things moving, simply contact our offices via our official e-mail address: **berry.al@thefuneralcompany.ca**
Fade to black, but with the e-mail address and website address remaining on screen the longest.	

About the Author

Matt Doyle is a speculative fiction author from the UK and identifies as pansexual and genderfluid. Matt has spent a great deal of time chasing dreams, a habit which has led to success in a great number of fields. To date, this has included spending ten years as a professional wrestler, completing a range of cosplay projects, and publishing multiple works of fiction.

These days, Matt can be found working on multiple novels and stories, blogging about pop culture, and plotting and planning far too many projects.

Email: mattdoylemedia@hotmail.com

Facebook: www.fb.me/MattDoyleMedia

Twitter: @mattdoylemedia

Website: www.mattdoylemedia.com

Other books by this author

The Cassie Tam Files

Addict

The Fox, the Dog and the King

LV48

Coming Soon from Matt Doyle

Half-Light

The Cassie Tam Files, Book Five

"*Diu.*"

I look to my right and find a free space to pull the car into. I have a couple of different ring tones on my cell phone, each assigned to give me a clear idea of whether I need—or want—to answer it. This generic-but-far-too-loud melody marks this call as coming from one particular number. Given what day it is, I've been expecting to hear from them. The last few days have been spent playing a game that's essentially the adult equivalent of passing notes in class. I leave a note somewhere, I get another at home, I respond somewhere else. It's been a pain, and it's all been leading up to this. "It's where it leads next I'm worried about."

I steel myself and tap the screen to answer the call. A female voice comes through, dripping with an overacted panic. "Is...is that Cassandra Tam?"

I recognize the voice instantly. "It is. Cassie or Caz is fine."

"My name is Anna Welch. I need help, Miss Tam."

I sigh. "Well, that's what I'm here for. Do you want to discuss this over the phone, or would you rather meet in person?"

"In person," she replies, and I can hear the smile in her voice. "Somewhere neutral would be best. I'm rather paranoid, you see."

"Okay, that's fine. Where?"

"I'll text you the location."

She hangs up, and the text comes through almost immediately. Once I've finished reading it, I can't help but smile. She wants to meet at an old abandoned warehouse. It's one I'm familiar with. A few months back, I broke up a dog fight in the same building. During the case, I discovered there's a secret entrance to the building via an underground network of hallways. *That* gives me a way to monitor her if I need to. Or a convenient escape route.

I hit the speed dial for Lori, and it goes straight to her answering service. After the beep, I say, "Hey, it's Cassie. I guess you're driving. Listen, I've just had a call from a potential client, and I'm gonna have to go meet with them. I'm still coming, but it may be worth checking what later times there are for the film, just in case this runs long. Anyway. Be with you soon."

I throw my phone onto the passenger seat next to me and pull out into the light traffic of the New Hopeland afternoon.

Also Available from NineStar Press

Connect with NineStar Press

www.ninestarpress.com

www.facebook.com/ninestarpress

www.facebook.com/groups/NineStarNiche

www.twitter.com/ninestarpress

www.tumblr.com/blog/ninestarpress